North Shore Rhapsody

By

Dee Alessandra

PublishAmerica
Baltimore

ISBN: 1-4241-2448-4
PUBLISHED BY PUBLISHAMERICA, LLLP
www.publishamerica.com
Baltimore

Printed in the United States of America

Mary Smith and Levy Garcia continue to offer endless computer lessons to me, their slowest student.

Heartfelt thanks to Pam Snow for her time and interest.

My husband, Len, is a good listener, an invaluable asset to an author.

Chapter 1

The bird flew north to south along the Bluff View shoreline. The sun was setting casting brilliant red-orange rays across the gently rippling waters of Lake Michigan. Swooping low over the country club, landing at the edge of a man-made pond hazard, it stillhunted, resting on its spindly, shiny black legs, sharp eyes darting at the slightest movement below the water's surface. It quickly bent its long graceful neck down to the water and came up with a tiny silver fish in its beak. Finally, the heron pushed with its awkward legs, spread its blue grey wings and lifted off splashing against the water, shaking down ruby droplets of shimmering water. Legs straight out behind it, wings flopping, slowly, strongly, neck elongated out in front, the majestic bird headed slowly toward the manicured gardens.

The heron's eye caught a glimmer of movement in the Randals' koi pond as it cleared the black roof top. It touched down in the reeds at the edge of the pond and swiftly took a young koi in its bill, shaking it, then gulping it down quickly.

James Randal sat on his deck and watched the heron. It looked back over its tucked wings and stared at the house. James zipped his jacket against the sudden gust of wind. The heron lifted majestically and headed toward the boat docks that lined the beaches of this affluent neighborhood. It landed on top of the cabin of the Boston Whaler called the 'Eva'. James stood, leaned on his cane, watched the bird for a few moments and felt incredibly sad. He wondered if people really can come back as other life forms. He read somewhere that people in India believed that cows were their dearly departed ancestors. He shrugged. At eighty nine one gets incredibly silly thoughts. Yet, from his deck, the heron on the 'Eva' looking back at him, well, he couldn't help thinking of Chet Romans. Chet loved that whaler and could never part with it. Until the day he died, he enjoyed watching friends take the boat out on fishing trips. He'd sit at the large window at the veterans' home and smile at the scene. He always got a wave, and he always waved back. Randal missed the fishing trips. He missed a lot of things. He sighed and went inside the sliding glass door. He stood at the door and stared out at the heron, still looking his way. The bird spread its wings and rose against the setting sun. Randal felt a little foolish, but he waved.

Chapter 2

Ada Venetti sat at her long, mahogany dining room table. The crystal chandelier sparkled overhead. She had graphs and spread sheets in front of her. Her glasses were low over her nose as she poured over the figures. Having recently received an offer for her garbage business from the city of Chicago, she was contemplating becoming an extremely rich woman. Carlie would be so proud, she thought. After all the grunt work in the early days, Carlie, Pete, and Chet built an empire, a legitimate empire. You boys made a lot of people filthy rich. She giggled to herself. AM Garbage. Ada and Muriel. How the guys wanted to put the girls' names on those first little trucks. They had to settle for their initials.

She smiled a broad smile. Look at all this. She wondered at the figures. Ada was well-organized having kept hospital records at the Veterans' Home for many, many years. Then, after her Carlie passed away, she had to get involved in AM. Her first husband, Pete Burkas, ran the small business with Chet and later, Carlie. The business expanded from central city to all points north, south, east and west. The routes got bigger, too.

Ridley and Ridley, she sighed. What would we do without them? First, George's dad, Greg. What a gem. He always knew what to do with any money Chet and Pete brought to him. They were like little boys. She put her hand on the spread sheets lovingly. So many good times. Now, I guess it really will come to an end.

Voices from the past crossed her mind. "Look what we found. What

7

should we do with it?" Greg always knew how to handle the dough, for four percent. Everyone got rich in the Chicago of the Twenties. The true worth of the Ridleys was manipulating and managing the money through the rough times. Sitting tight during the panics. Financially avoiding the chaos. George quietly followed his father's lead and expertly stepped in when Greg passed away.

Ada dialed George's number and asked him to stop in on his way to the office. He said he'd be there in a half hour. Ada made coffee and set one end of the table with breakfast dishes. She went into the kitchen and asked cook to make breakfast for two.

"Mr. Ridley likes omelets, Kate, and that thick toast you do so well."

"Yes, Ada. He likes the mushroom and onion omelet. I'll get on it right now."

"How long have you been cooking for us Kate?" Ada fingered the pearls around her neck.

Kate smiled. She was short, wiry, and full of sixty-year old energy. She nodded her head at Ada, "About fifteen years for you and Carlie. The last three just for you and me. But we're easy, right? It's like I'm stealing my pay check. You eat like a bird."

"Even a bird has to eat right, though. You seem to make the food we always like to eat."

"I learned from the best. You don't work for Muriel Karetsky and not learn to cook, and bake. Six years at the Lakeside Inn taught me a lot about cooking, baking and serving."

"We were lucky Muriel let you go. I do believe you helped Carlie so much with his nutrition. He wouldn't eat for anyone but you. You had such a good way with him. I'm grateful to you, Kate." She tossed her head, "But, now, we have some company coming."

George came into Ada's dining room. He was tall, steel grey hair waved neatly back, tailored navy suit with a navy and gold striped tie, white shirt stiffly visible at his neck and wrists.

He hugged Ada warmly. "You look terrific in light blue, Ada." Her hair was still dark, streaked lightly with grey. She wore it simply, short, curled and pushed back. Diamond earrings flashed, her dark eyes shiny with tears.

"Forgive me, George. Any ties with the past and I well up with the waterworks." She dabbed her eyes with a tissue. "How have you been?"

"We're all well. Kids are doing fine in school. Vacations are over for now. The Mrs. wants to go to the islands in January, but that's a busy time for me." He held her at arms length. "You should go with her, Ada. Close up and take two weeks in Cancun or Aruba. Be nice for you."

"I'll think about it. Let's eat first. I'm kind of hungry."

Kate came out with a tray of toast, butter, jam and juice. George went over to her as she placed the tray on the table.

""Kate, my favorite cook." He hugged her. "Can I steal you away from Ada?"

"Never, George, never. But I'll enjoy cooking for you whenever you're here visiting us. We wish it was more often, right Ada? Now, let me bring on your favorite omelet."

"I'm in heaven. Two beauties and my favorite food," George smiled.

They ate, talked about the neighborhood, the shoreline improvements, taxes and travels. George leaned back as Kate poured more coffee. He patted his stomach.

"I'm full. I'll need a nap by eleven. But, unfortunately, I have a busy day ahead of me. Now, Ada, what can I do for you?"

She stood up. "Let's move to this end of the table." She gestured at the papers spread out on the opposite end.

He walked over and stared down. "Your spread sheets from AM. I'm familiar with all this Ada. What's different?"

She picked up a stapled set of blue eleven by fourteens. "Know what this is?"

"Looks like a contract or a proposal," he squinted at the sheets in her hand. "What is it?"

"George, the city wants to buy me out. They have a sanitation department but they want it to include the entire city garbage package which means pick up, disposal, barges, special trucks to transport out of state to dump sites, and so on. I can't keep up with the regulations any more."

"What do you think, Ada? You ready?"

"I think so. It was easy before, but now with the city commissions mandates and the EPA, it's getting more and more difficult to handle. I have a good staff but sometimes I feel lost in all the do's and don'ts. You know all about the finances, George. Now I have to look to you as a friend, for your honest financial opinion."

"May I see the proposal?" he reached out his hand. They sat at the table as he quietly read over the city's offer. Ada turned to the window and looked out over the docks. She thought of Pete and Chet. She was with both of them when their times came and she missed them both. They were such good friends, war buddies. Two busted up old soldiers, as Chet was fond of saying. Two men with a purpose, right or wrong who knew how to make money, hide money and use money to make the people around them happy. She watched a heron make its way over the docks, across the lawn and swoop up over her deck. How beautiful, she thought. She looked back at George bent over the contract.

He thought it was a good contract. But like a true Ridley, he was his father's son, he knew he could negotiate more.

"Ada, let me draft a counter offer for you. I'll bring it back tonight for you to sign. Then we'll see what happens."

"That's fine, George. I knew you'd be a big help. Your father was a gem, too, you know."

"Now, I need to go. I'll see you this afternoon at the board meeting?"

"I'll be there. It should be a happy meeting. Are the others all set to attend?" Ada asked.

"Yes, it should be a fun hour or so. I'm looking forward to it." He shrugged into his coat, called a bye-bye to Kate, and left.

Kate cleared the table. Ada was thoughtful. She wandered into the kitchen. "Kate, how would you like to take a trip?"

"Ada?"

"Like a cruise to the islands, maybe? And we could go on to the Panama Canal. I always wanted to see how they get those huge ships through those locks."

Kate laughed. "Let's get packing."

Chapter 3

The little red light on the camera went out. Jan Harcher removed the thin headset and put it on the desk in front of her. She just signed off as anchor for the news program 'A Fresh Spin'. She smiled at her partner as she rose and left the set.

"See you at eleven, Jim."

"Have a good one. See you later." Jim made a few notes and also left the set until the eleven o'clock news.

Jan Ryerson Harcher made her way to her car. She was a strikingly beautiful woman, tall, thin, long blond loose hair, good skin and white, even teeth. She had everything she needed for camera close-ups. After years of photo journalism all over the world, she had the experienced, confident demeanor of a reporter who covered the news well. She adjusted the rear-view mirror, checked her hair, ran her hand gently over her face and leaned back against the headrest. She needed a moment. She closed her eyes. Kevin, she thought. She wished he could be here, going to Ridley's office with her. You'd get such a kick out of all this, Kev. She smiled sadly.

Kevin and Jan Harcher had been freelance correspondents. A couple who loved reporting on the edge. They did it well and were in constant demand. Jan's photos won awards and Kevin's relaxed informal approach to reporting resulted in revealing interviews and exciting, close-to-the-action footage. He met Janice at Ridley's office and knew immediately that they clicked. He persuaded her to marry him and she did. He adopted her son, Brian and they were an instant family. Brian became a well-traveled, well-adjusted youngster who appreciated his parents' calling. He proudly displayed their pictures and articles on the cork board in his room. Grandma Judy and Brian never missed their TV coverage of events in far away places.

Until Viet Nam. The Delta, and the loss of Kevin.

They flew low over the rice paddy, the rotors stirring up the water. A single sniper bullet pierced the Plexiglas windshield, continued up and hit the rotor mechanism. The pilot struggled with the controls, the body of the helicopter began to rock and spin. It crashed into the side of a low hill.

Jan flew from her assignment in South Africa to Saigon to accompany Kevin's body to Chicago. She spent months in relative silence, visiting his gravesite almost daily, thinking of all they had done, not wanting to let go of the closeness she still felt.

A warm, sunny morning in June, looking out over the lake. Jan smiled. Then she chuckled at the memory of Kevin taking her out on Chet's boat, the 'Eva', cutting the motor and making passionate love to her as the boat rocked gently side to side, up and down, smoothly, rhythmically, back and forth, back and forth, side to side.

Kevin whispered into her ear, "We're rocking the boat."

She moaned in pleasure.

"Marry me Janice?"

"Yes, you know I will. You know I want to."

After months of mourning, Jan went to Kevin's gravesite to say goodbye. Then she accepted the long-standing offer to anchor the news show, 'A Fresh Spin'. She spoke to Kevin, told him about her new job and thanked him for her name.

"Three syllables, kid. Janice Ryerson is too long. Leslie Stahl, three syllables. Tom Brokaw, three syllables, Jan Harcher, three syllables. You have to marry me for the name."

She did, and it was right. She opened her eyes, backed out of the station parking lot and headed for George Ridley's office.

Chapter 4

The Lakeside Inn was one of a chain of four restaurants in the Greater Chicago area. All were owned by Muriel and Jozef Karetsky. Jozef learned to bake and cook at his parents' tiny restaurant and catering business in Central Chicago back in the 1920's. Their business thrived with private parties on the north shore at the stately homes of the wealthy such as Chet Romans, Pete and Ada Burkas, the Randals, the Ingrahms and the Harchers. When Muriel arrived at the Karetskys, she was so eager to learn and Jozef was so impressed by her beauty, her love of fine food, her singing voice, it was just a matter of time before the two fell hopelessly in love. When she baked with him, he not only taught her the skills he knew, he also taught her how to relax, how to react to disasters in the kitchen, how to laugh. By the time she struck out on her own, he couldn't help but follow her to her first two establishments, worked with her side by side, and then they married. Muriel not only needed his guidance, she also needed his unconditional love and attention. Jozef stole Muriel away from Chet Romans, her financial backer and, mostly absentee lover. Muriel and Jozef went on to open four successful restaurants, raised two fine children, and along the way Muriel was offered a contract to cut five albums of songs from the 20's and 30's, one of which went platinum.

After Jozef died of heart failure at age 72, Muriel hired four dedicated managers for the restaurants and slowed down to occasional visits, private parties and meetings. All receipts were picked up and taken to the offices of Ridley and Ridley Associates.

The Lakeside Inn was Muriel's favorite. It jutted out alongside a dock like a fishing boat. Patrons could eat by the windows on the three sides of the dining room and watch boats pushing out to fish or water ski, and boats docking with their catches or tanned water sports lovers.

She entered the lobby of the Lakeside. Judy Ryerson, her manager was at the desk greeting and seating diners.

"Muriel," Judy smiled. "Eating lunch here today?" She looked at her watch. It was only eleven.

"Yes, Judy. With you, okay? By the last window, okay? Get Robin to cover for you. Want to?"

Judy signaled for the pert waitress to come over. "Robin, get the early comers in. I'll be back after I have some lunch with Mrs. Karetsky. Thanks."

"You really like working, Judy?" Muriel asked as they sat at the round table near the window. The sun glanced off the water surface and reflected into the wide dining room. It looked magical to Judy. She felt good working at the Lakeside.

"I go nuts in that big house all alone. Jan is either at the studio or at the cemetery and Brian is involved in so many projects I can't keep up. I feel sort of left out. We could have stayed in Chet's house after she and Kevin were married. They were hardly home anyway. But, they wanted a home of their own. I love it, but it's just so big." Judy sighed.

"It's a beautiful home. Wish Kevin could have enjoyed it more. She misses him a lot doesn't she?" The waitress served coffees.

"You know, Muriel, lately she's been better. She has even skipped going to the cemetery a few times. I think she has finally come to terms with her past," Judy took a sip of her coffee.

"When she opens up to you, you'll know she's accepted it all," Muriel said.

"So," Judy looked at Muriel. "Are you ready for the meeting this afternoon?"

"That's what I wanted to talk to you about. Will you be there?" Muriel asked.

"I know we don't have to be, but why should George Ridley have all the fun? Sure, I'll be there. I guess I'll get the same kick as when Chet Romans changed Jan's life all around." Judy pursed her lips. She seemed to want to say more. Instead, she looked at Muriel.

Muriel looked back at Judy. "What?"

"Nothing," Judy said. "You like this salad? It's your new one. Chicken chunks over a lettuce, spinach salad with a vinaigrette dressing."

"I like the idea of not having to handle a sandwich. It's different, also filling. How is it going?"

"Great. The ladies love it. Probably for that reason. Goes well with tea, too. We sell a lot of tea at lunchtime." Her voice trailed off.

"Look," Muriel said. "Tell me what's bothering you."

"Okay. You're here for lunch on a day when we have an afternoon meeting with the Ridleys. You're also looking at me like you're trying to unlock a secret. Did we both get a call we weren't supposed to get?"

"Yes, I did. From one of the female candidates," Muriel said quietly. "She knew she wasn't supposed to, but I guess she was going for broke. Wanted to know if I understood everything in her application, was her paper work all right, she mostly wanted to know if she should even attend the meeting."

"What did you tell her?" asked Judy with an emphasis on the 'you'.

"Probably the same thing you'd tell her if she had called you. I told her she was lucky enough to be one of the final five and she should be present," Muriel shrugged.

"It was one of the young men who called me. He wanted to know if there was something more he could do. I got the impression that George Ridley didn't tell these five scholarship candidates everything they should know." Judy looked worried.

"Well, I think you're right. We were made to understand the screening process, but the finalists were left in the dark. I'm sure that they think this meeting with the Romans-Burkas foundation is one more step to the final choice of a candidate. I think Ridley failed to tell them that they are all the choice. Of course, the Ridleys always were a funny group. Greg played everything close to the vest and more than anything else, he loved a big surprise, a good laugh and a tricky deal."

Judy wiped her lips with a napkin, "It should be an interesting and emotional meeting. I, for one, know how their parents, guardians, whoever, are going to react. I'll never forget my own amazement when Jan found Chet Romans' cryptic note that gave Jan, Brian and me a full, rewarding life. He gave us everything."

Muriel leaned over and patted Judy's hand. "Me too, Judy. Me too.

Chapter 5

Over the years, Ridley and Ridley Associates acquired offices on both sides of the Sherman Bank Building. They now occupied the entire south half of the building's first floor. The bank was located on the north half with a marble lobby in between.

George's financial firm boasted a beautifully decorated waiting area, three conference rooms and seven private offices. George's office was strategically located in the front with the traffic and hustle bustle of the inner city as his backdrop. The atmosphere was hushed, lavish with thick carpeting and low lighting.

George had his assistant set coffee thermoses along the long conference table. Note pads were lined up along the gleaming table. He put out white coffee mugs, plates of pastries and black pens. George set the thermostat 68 degrees. The foundation board was scheduled to arrive at two, the candidates at two thirty. George smiled to himself. *Five new clients someday, if all goes well. May they all end up as filthy rich as their benefactors.* goes well.

Chapter 6

The Randals and the Ingrahms drove down from Bluff View together. They munched on pastries as they waited, talking softly of how they shouldn't be eating the sweets. Randal did not look well.

"Are you comfortable, Jim? Want the heat up or down?" George voiced his concern.

"I'll be fine, George. Feels pretty good in here, actually." He took his wife's hand. "We've been looking forward to your little dog and pony show all week."

Muriel breezed in, chiffon scarf trailing behind her. She was tall and lovely as usual. They all hugged. Ada came in behind her followed by Judy and Jan. They chatted, taking seats around the table. The Harchers were the last to arrive. They sat next to Jan. She leaned into them for a quiet hug.

George began. He welcomed them, spoke briefly of the generosity of the foundation members. The roots of the money and the hard work that went into the creation of their individual fortunes was one of George's favorite subjects..

He began to speak of the financial mission of the board when Muriel interrupted him.

"George, do these kids know they're already picked, that the process for them is over?" She raised her eyebrows at him.

He coughed and ran his finger around his collar. "No. They think this is the final step and that one of them will be picked for the full scholarship."

Ada said, "That's cruel."

"Trust me, Ada. Have I ever led any of you wrong? Did my father? I'm doing what I feel he would have done, or advised me to do, in this situation. I have given this a lot of thought. We want people who can stand a little pressure. This won't kill them. And think of their elation when they finally realize that they all made it." He smiled a toothy grin, put his fingertips together and said to them all, "Ready?"

They all nodded and waited while George left the room to get the five college freshmen who applied, along with a few thousand others, to the Romans-Burkas scholarship foundation.

Carl Ingrahms leaned forward in his seat. "I'm pretty excited. I've been on a number of boards, usually construction looking at bids. I've never been involved in a scholarship process. I guess this one is unusual because after the initial weeding out, we are getting to meet the five winners. But they don't know that they've won. I like Ridley's style. These kids will never forget this moment, will they?"

"Our foundation is unique, Carl. This one is quite different. I like it. I'm sure Chet and Pete would heartily approve." Randal laughed loudly as he removed his jacket. "Sally, give me a hand, would you?"

"Are you all right, dear?" She helped him remove his jacket and placed it over the back of his chair.

"I'm fine. Just a little overanxious and excited. Relax, dear." He patted her hand gently.

Muriel knit her brows together. Her long black hair turned stylishly around her shoulders. She put her cheek on her hand, "God, they are going to faint dead away when the relief hits them. I hope George knows what he's doing. Right to the final screening, he let them think there was one more step. That we were the ones who would pick that lucky, final candidate."

Jan Harcher laughed. "Wish I could have a camera crew in here. Talk about human interest and raw emotion. I wish...."

Fran Harcher leaned toward Jan and put her arm around her

shoulders. "We do too, dear. He would have appreciated all the high drama." She smiled warmly at her daughter-in-law.

They all nodded. Time was moving them all along. Their fortunes were made and in place and about to help others the way they were once financially jolted by Pete Burkas or Chet Romans.

George opened the paneled oak door and gestured the three males and two females into the room. He was beaming.

Leading the line was Marie Maneros, petite, shiny black hair pulled back, a few stray hairs framing her serious, oval face, her dark brown eyes wide, not quite knowing where to look. Marie wore a dark grey jacket and skirt, dark stockings and black, sensible heels. Her white, high-necked blouse looked freshly pressed.

Behind her stood Amy Crowley, tall, curly chestnut hair, flashing green eyes, thin lips, no makeup. Amy wore a brown, long, soft paisley skirt with a tan jacket. She and Marie sat at the end of the long table.

Hal Jensen exuded confidence. He had soft brown and blonde curls that tumbled over his forehead and around his ears. He was deeply tanned and muscular. His blue eyes smiled at the group along with his flashy grin. Immediately likeable, he nodded to everyone and sat next to Marie. He adjusted his tweed jacket, reached over and patted her hand.

The last two students came into the conference room, looked around tentatively and sat across from the others at the end of the table. Sam Carter, Afro-American, broad shouldered, medium height, hair neatly short but curly, great smile, nodded to the panel. He wore a blue dress shirt open at the collar, navy sport coat and khaki pants. On his right sat Barry Kretzler, short, thin, with wiry black hair and a face made paler by his dark, thick eyebrows and deep, almost black, eyes. His thin lips were forced into a smile that was almost a grimace. He kept his hands in his lap, his back straight, shoulders slightly hunched up.

They were all tense, the board noted. It was palpable, and thick. Ada couldn't wait for George to put these boys and girls at ease. She glanced over at Muriel who stared at the five. Muriel looks so stern, Ada thought. Jim and Carl just look old, like me. She smiled a bit. The

Harchers look tragic. Except for Jan. She's looking great these days. Ada wondered if the period of grief was finally coming to an end. She also wondered how the board looked to the five candidates. Like a bunch of old fogies, I'll bet.

George walked around the table and put fat file folders in front of each candidate. Their names stood out starkly, white letters against royal blue. They each stared at their own folders. No one reached out to open them.

He began. "I'd first like to introduce you to the board members of the Romans-Burkas Scholarship Foundation. Each of these fine people were in some way helped along in their lives by Pete Burkas or Chet Romans, two men who were veterans of World War 1 and, by various twists and turns of fate and hard work and luck, built a financial empire in the 1920's and 1930's here in Chicago. The board feels that now they would like to pass on some of their good fortune to others who need a financial hand. You five have been screened, and processed and rated and whatever else the college people do to identify those who fit the qualifications of various grants and award programs. You have all demonstrated extraordinary talent and ability. They tell us that you five best met the requirements of our application process. So, we will all read your folders and poke around in your backgrounds at our leisure. Your folders will remain in my office to be read by your benefactors. First, I'd like to introduce you to board member Carl Ingrahms. Carl?"

Barry Kretzler raised his hand. Ridley nodded at him. "Mr. Ridley, when will we know if we have been selected if the board has not yet done their background check?"

George reddened. There were smiles around the table, nods of heads. Ridley was caught with his hand in the cookie jar. He coughed, "Soon, Barry. Very soon. It shouldn't take too long at all. Carl?"

Ingrahms stood, congratulated the candidates and told them how Pete and Chet were instrumental in helping him get the veterans' memorial home idea off and running. How Chet Romans died in the first home in Chicago. He told them he was proud to be a part of the foundation.

Jim Randal remained seated. He spoke of the generosity of the two men. He closed his eyes for a moment and reflected on Chet Romans' love of fine watches and fine cars and how glad he was to be part of a foundation that could do so much good.

Harcher rose slowly. "Chet Romans brought much happiness to my family, especially our son. He brought us Jan, here. She and Kevin covered history around the world. Jan is still doing it. Our contribution to the foundation will always be in Kevin Harcher's name. Good luck to all of you."

"Ada?" urged George.

She glanced sideways at George. "George and I don't always agree," she muttered. "I'll have plenty to say later. Right now, as Pete Burkas' wife, welcome to the foundation. May you benefit as much as we all did by knowing Pete Burkas and Chet Romans."

Muriel leaned back in her chair. "I guess I've been where you are. You wouldn't be here if you didn't need a lift. I don't know yet what your backgrounds are, but, Ada, Jan, and I would have ended up a whole lot differently if it weren't for Pete and Chet. Also, those two men may have gone in a different direction if it weren't for the wise counsel of the Ridleys. Welcome and good luck."

George stood again, cleared his throat and started, "Just a few details...."

They all noticed the five reach out to hold hands around the table. They were all ready to support each other.

Muriel got up and went to the window.

Ada said, "George?"

Jan held her pen to her lips and spoke softly into it, "And now ladies and gentlemen, a fresh spin on today's news."

Everyone on the board chuckled. George blushed and said, "Oh, all right. I'll go out of order."

The five candidates looked confused. Marie bent her head down and held Hal's hand tightly. Amy was sitting straight and tall in her chair, staring at the folder in front of her.

George smiled, finally, and said, with raised brows, "You five finalists are just that. The final five. The five students who will benefit from the Romans-Burkas Foundation. Not just one of you, but all of you."

There was silence in the room. Marie Maneros was the first to speak. "We all win?"

George nodded, "Yes, dear. You all win."

Amy sank back in her chair, still holding hands. She raised both her hands, as did the others, still holding on to each other. Hal's cheeks were wet. Barry Kretzler looked over at the board and mouthed "Thank you."

"Since the foundation board understands the inner workings of this scholarship, perhaps they can go on to dinner. We'll join you in about a half hour." George helped Jim into his jacket and walked them all to the door.

Jan Harcher waved on her way out. "See you all later." Judy was still wiping her eyes with a tissue.

George closed the door and turned to the table. "It's simple and I'll be brief then we can join them at the Lakeside Inn for dinner. Now, you know you were chosen on the basis of your drive, your grades and your need. However, one of our criteria was that you did get yourselves through the first year of college. You are all enrolled in a college close to where you live so that you do not need to live on campus. Under this scholarship, you choose the university that will give you the best education in your field. I strongly advise you to live on campus. All educational expenses will be paid by the foundation. Your signature and an account number will be forwarded to this office. If you lift the cover of your folder you'll find a card in a leather holder. Your account number is on the card. Use it to purchase anything you need on campus. My phone number is on the back of the card. Call this office whenever you feel the need."

"When you say we can go to the school of our choice, does that include ivy league?" Sam Carter couldn't keep the tremor out of his voice.

"Son, that includes Oxford if you're so inclined," George said. "I will need to know your choice, however, by the end of this month so I can get you all enrolled and paid up for your sophomore year. The same will be true of the junior and senior years. You must keep in touch with me if you plan any changes in your school. Your scholarship extends to one year beyond your senior graduation. During that time, we can sit down and see where you are. The foundation board felt that a yearly allotment would help with any expenses that may arise that would make your life difficult. So you now each have an account with me for fifty thousand dollars. These accounts will receive an additional fifty thousand each year until the scholarship runs out. Please be discreet. Your money is nobody's business. Speaking of it may lead to social problems. Probably, the less said the better. Pay your bills, do your assignments and so on and you should all be fine."

"Do you get paid by the foundation?" Marie Maneros asked.

"Yes, I do. My fee is four percent of any deposits made to this firm. That was a perceptive question, Marie. I will be taking four percent of your yearly account money. However, I will be managing your money, investing it and making it work for you. You will earn far more than the four percent that I take initially. You should be financially stable enough to either start out in your field or go on further in school. When you want to use your personal account, you'll need to call me or one of my assistants, explain what you need and why, and it will be sent on to you."

Barry Kretzler cleared his throat, "I can't find words to express what I feel about what happened to us here today, and I'm deeply appreciative. But, it's kind of a controlling system, isn't it?"

"Yes, Barry, and believe me, some day you'll thank me the way the folks you met here today continue to thank this firm. Money demands control and it's what we do here and we do it well. Trust me. I will take on the responsibility of managing your money. You're now free to pursue your career. I'm not unreasonable. I realize there will be needs that must be met. Just let us keep it all within reasonable parameters."

Silence.

"Fine." George reached into his inside jacked pocket and drew out five envelopes which he quickly passed around. "There is two thousand dollars in each envelope. Enough to get you back home to finish your freshman year and to get you through the summer."

Amy Crowley peered inside the envelope, laid it on the table and said, "I'll work this summer, full time. I work part time three nights a week at a photo lab. I'll be able to quit at the end of the summer and concentrate on school. This scholarship will save my father's life. He's working two jobs now trying to get me through school." Her voice broke. "Speaking for myself, I feel so lucky, there just aren't the right words to express it."

The others nodded in agreement. "Here, here," said Hal Jensen. "There are four kids in my family. My folks look on college as a luxury, simply because they are overwhelmed at having to educate all of us. I've been working, too. With a roofer who keeps me on during the school year when the weather allows. It will be so nice to be able to put school first for a change. Since I'm the oldest, perhaps I will be able to help my siblings a bit, too. I want to work this summer because my boss is so busy."

George said, "I'll get my assistant to help me get us all to the Lakeside. The others want to spend some time with you. By the way, were you comfortable last night at the Romans' house?"

They agreed that the accommodations were more than adequate. George put up a finger, "By the way, you all purchased bus or train tickets to Chicago. We appreciate that you gave up your spring break to come here. We also know that you either saved up or borrowed to buy your tickets. Give them to my secretary and she will reimburse you the full price for the round trip.

Hal Jensen turned visibly red. He looked embarrassed. "How do I get back to Brownsville, Texas if I don't have a train ticket?" The others looked equally confused.

George reached into his sport coat pocket and came out with a clenched fist. He lay five sets of keys on the table. "When we get to the Lakeside Inn, you'll find five baby Buicks in the lot. They are all the same, except for color. May I choose?"

No one answered. They looked at each other and couldn't stop grinning. Sam Carter said, "Nobody move. I do not want to wake up."

Marie Maneros whispered, "Not yet, anyway. It feels too good."

"Marie, surely you'll be happy with powder blue. Amy, definitely the champagne. Hal, you'll look great in red. Sam, forest green should satisfy you. And, Barry, white with a red interior should be just fine for you." He pushed over the keys one by one and said, "What do you think?"

Amy got up and stepped over to George. She put up her arms, placed them around his neck and kissed his cheek. Hal gave George a warm handshake and a hug. Marie snuggled against George's ample chest. Barry and Sam, too hugged the big man. George was blushing and smiling. "Just don't let us down. You are an experiment as well as a tax write-off. Five years from now I hope we're all just as happy as we are right now at this moment. Perhaps when you are all situated and making tons of money, as Ridley clients, you, too, will become members of the board.

They left in two cars and went on to the Lakeside Inn. Judy Ryerson greeted them at the door. Everyone was smiling. She led the group down an aisle of tables to a long table set up by a large window overlooking the harbor. Amy and Marie stood at the window and watched two fishing boats set out, leaving a white wake behind them. The sun was setting, the scene was lovely.

Muriel joined them by the window. "Peaceful, isn't it?"

I live in central Pennsylvania so anytime I see water, I appreciate it. This is spectacular," said Marie.

Amy squinted, "Is that a Boston Whaler moored out there? I've seen them on Lake Erie. I live outside of Buffalo."

"Yes, it is." Muriel looked out at the *Eva*. "It's an old one. It once belonged to Chet Romans. We've all used it from time to time. Feel free to vacation here and use the boat. Bring your father. I'm sure he'd enjoy some good fishing."

Sam Carter came over and looked at the scene. "What kind of bird is that out there? The one on the pier."

Jim Randal leaned sideways on his chair to get a look. "That's a blue heron. He's been around a while now. He's a good fisherman."

Just then the heron put its head straight down and dove like a lightning bolt into the water.

"It got a fish," Marie squealed with delight.

"Show off," muttered Randal under his breath.

They ordered and ate and chatted with each other. The five heard the phenomenal stories of Chet's eccentric generosities. They told the board about their backgrounds and goals.

There was a flurry at the reservation desk. Judy hustled down the aisle and came back towing the tall, blonde, handsome Jack Kacinski and his beautiful wife, Regina.

"Sorry we're late. The plane was early but the traffic from the airport was horrendous at this hour."

"Oh, my gosh," gasped Marie. "You're the governor of Pennsylvania."

"And, also, more importantly, one of the board members of the Romans-Burkas foundation," he said proudly.

George looked sheepish, "Sorry, Jack. I neglected to tell them that. There was so much to go over."

"That's fine, George. We're just glad to be a part of all this. Are we too late to eat?" He looked around the table.

Judy raised her hand and a waitress came over immediately to take their order.

Jack regaled them with his own stories of Chet and his Uncle Joe. They laughed so hard at Uncle Joe stuffing money into bottles and burying them.

Sam wiped his eyes and said, "Here we are struggling to get through community colleges and your uncle is up there in Pennsylvania filling old wine bottles with cash. Did you ever find out where that money came from?"

Everyone turned to Jack. "No, son, we never did. It's one of life's imponderables. Like, where would Chet have been if he didn't listen to Pete Burkas and go to Chicago instead of staying in Morgantown and ending up in the mines. We can only guess where their money came from. Before their garbage business, they were a part of Chicago where a lot of fortunes were made because of the thing called prohibition. They were a part of this city's historical past. We'll never know. But, if not for them, where would we be?"

"Amen," said Marie.

The group lingered over coffee. Jim Randal rose first. He leaned on his cane. He looked tired. "Good night all, and lots of good luck to you youngsters. You make us proud now. They left slowly ambling toward the lobby. All five got up and surrounded Randal, shaking his hand. By now they knew that Randal, with his Detroit connections, was instrumental in their gift cars.

The Ingrahms also wished everyone a good night. They told the five to stay in touch, not just with George but with the board, too. Carl invited them to Bluff View whenever they could make it. He reminded them that the Romans' house was usually available, and if not, they were welcome to stay at the Ingrahms.

Jack and Regina were finishing their dinner. Jack turned to Hal Jensen and said, "Are you all staying at the Romans' house tonight?"

"Tonight and tomorrow night, too. We have another meeting with George tomorrow, then Saturday morning we'll have to get back to begin the end of our freshman year. He wants us to identify our school choices for September," Hal explained. "He said he thought we had enough time to think of the school we wanted to attend. I'm sure we can transfer if we change our minds. Now is a good time to come up with a place. I am dead sure I want to go to MIT."

Marie leaned over and spoke around Hal, "There is an extra bedroom if you want to stay over. I won't use mine. I've been sleeping on the sun porch."

Sam laughed, "Marie can't get enough of the water view."

"As a Pennsylvanian, I can appreciate that," Jack smiled.

"You're always welcome at my house, Jack," reminded Ada.

"Mine, too. I only have one grandchild with me this week," Muriel said. "I have three empty bedrooms and Ada has four. So, take your pick."

"Thanks, both of you, but if the group at Chet's doesn't mind, we'd like to stay over with them. I don't know why, but I sleep really well there."

It was settled. The party broke up. In the parking lot, everyone gathered around the new cars, laughed and joked about the colors. Muriel and Marie hung back a little.

"I'm so glad one of you is a music major," Muriel told Marie.

"Since I was little I loved to hear it and tried to figure out how it worked. We couldn't afford lessons but I spent all the time I could in my high school music department. I've heard all your albums on my radio, Muriel. I could listen forever."

"Thank you. I'm making one more. My last. Songs of the '20's. It's getting harder to maintain the tone, you know."

"I'm so glad to have met you. Suddenly all my dreams are coming true. All in one day. My grandparents took me in when my parents died. They're postal workers and their wages would be enough to keep them comfortable, but trying to get me through Julliard would be a tremendous burden. Now, maybe they'll be able to live their own lives, travel and visit some of our relatives in Puerto Rico."

Muriel smiled, "Good night, Marie. Please keep me posted. All five of you are such good choices. Pete and Chet would get such a kick out of all this."

Jack and Regina sat up late with the group. They listened to Jack's stories of Chet, how Chet was shunned by Morgantown because they thought he returned from WW1 France with syphilis. Living alone in a shack in the woods on the fringe of the town Chet made frequent trips to Pete in Chicago where the two were carving out their own empire.

"Money was nothing to these men," Jack said. "It was the acquisition of money that gave them a jolt, a kick. Finding a suitcase full, grabbing it out of a disaster, cramming it into safe deposit boxes, bags, bottles, concrete root cellars. That was where their fun was. They prided themselves for always being in the right place at the right time and knowing how to handle the situation. Then when they got older they enjoyed giving it away. Especially Chet. There was so much, and thanks to Ridley's arithmetic and common sense, it attained a life of its own. He manipulated it around two depressions, one really big one, a couple of wars and like Pete and Chet, Greg Ridley managed to have their money in the right places at the right time."

Barry Kretzler sipped a cola, "So you would advise us to keep our money forever with George Ridley?"

"Chet first used the Krimsleys in Haileytown, Pennsylvania. Same smarts as the Ridleys. These men are worth their weight in gold and hard to find. Chet led me to the Krimsleys and I not only invested with them, I went to work for them and married into the firm. Without Krimsley, I would have never studied finances, ran for office or became governor of the state. I couldn't have thought my way through my uncle's money or what to do with it."

Amy was wide-eyed. "You mean you weren't motivated to go to school?"

"Not until I met Krimsley. He showed me the importance of manipulating money. He offered me a job and I knew after three months that if I was going to stay out of the coal mines, I needed to get some education. Honestly, when Chet first showed me my uncle's bottles, the first thing I thought of was a car. I saw myself in a big, shiny, new car. There wasn't a sensible thought in my head."

"So you had the money to attend finance school and then you had enough to run for various offices all the way up to governor. I'm impressed," said Sam.

"Well," Jack laughed, "when Chet moved on to Chicago permanently, he gave me six briefcases full of cash. I quickly deposited it all with the Krimsley firm. It's still there growing and multiplying. Ridley's the same way. Managing money is their life. So, to answer your question, Barry. When you're finished with the scholarship, stay put with the Ridleys and keep adding some of your fortune to their firm. You'll be paid back tenfold. What they do best is worry about your money for you. After all, you are going to be way to busy to get involved in money management."

"Phew," Amy stretched out her long legs. "I never thought that one day I'd say that I'm tired of listening to a long discussion about what to do with my money. But right now all I want to do is go lie down and think about it. And think and think and think."

Everyone laughed. Jack asked, "Have you called your parents or guardians yet?"

"No," Sam said. "I want to tell my parents face to face. I don't know what I could possibly say on the phone that will be convincing or believable."

"Me, too," Barry frowned. "My Mom will need me to make sure she's sitting down."

Hal agreed. "I can't wait. But I need to be the one to tell my folks that the pressure is off, that everything's going to be all right. I can't even imagine them without worries about money. That's always been their number one priority."

Amy asked, "Do you know what George meant when he said to be discreet, that there could be some problems in our lives?"

Jack got up and went to the window. "Money is a funny thing. It's like a presence that is screaming to be heard, but if you do that, the people around you may not understand. If you think about it and put yourself in your friends' places, there could be resentment at your good fortune. Money does strange things to the minds of others. It first creates a reaction of happiness at your good fortune, then it's a wish-it-were-me thought, finally, why her, or him instead of me. I'm telling you from experience. My colleagues tried real hard to trace the source of my campaign funds. Best advice is to talk about what your plans are, not how you're going to pay for them. Let that all be between you and the Ridleys." Jack stretched.

"Thank you, Governor. Good advice," Marie said softly.

"Now, Regina and I are going to bed. We have a ten a.m. flight back to Harrisburg tomorrow morning. I'm happy we had this chance to interact. The board will be interested in your progress, so, please, keep in touch with all of us. We need to see how much more the foundation money can do for five bright, driven stars such as yourselves."

Lights went out in the five bedrooms. Marie settled herself on the wicker sofa on the sun porch, leaned over and put out the lamp. It was so quiet here at night, mist hanging over the water like a soft veil. She watched the tiny dots of lights way out in the dark waters moving slowly along the horizon. Probably fishing boats. Closer, at the docks, an overhead halogen pole light shone down on the community dock. There were actually four or five of the lights along the boardwalk back of the one closest to shore. She could barely make out a heron standing on a log piling, one leg tucked up high, long graceful neck drooped under its wing. She drifted off to sleep.

Chapter 7

"So, any questions?" asked George as he leaned over the papers spread out on the conference table.

Marie was the first to respond. "I just want to be sure, Mr. Ridley...."

"Please, call me George, and with confidence. Remember, I work for you now."

She blushed, tucked an errant strand of curly black hair behind her ear. "Come September there will be a place for me at Julliard. They know about my major and they are prepared to accept me?"

"Just present yourself to admissions and settle in. They will assign you a dorm and a list of materials you'll need. That's true of everyone. Hal is all set at MIT, Sam at UCLA, Barry and Amy at Harvard. You're on full scholarship and the schools already have their money, paperwork is complete. It was simply a matter of electronically transferring funds."

Sam wanted to know about making purchases over the summer.

"Figure out what you'll need, call me and I'll get the money out to you promptly. Any check I send you will be against your account. You're all starting out with fifty. First year expenses will probably be the highest, but each successive year we'll be adding fifty to what you didn't spend the year before. At the end of five years you should all have enough for a decent career start. I'll worry about that, though and I'll let you know if I think you're being frivolous."

Chapter 8

Amy sat across from her father at the small kitchen table. Their Levittown cape cod sat on a cul-de-sac off one of the main arteries into Buffalo. She got home at eleven the night before, pulled into the short driveway and entered the quiet, dark house. Her dad was sleeping soundly. He was working two jobs so was usually tired.

She buttered her slice of whole wheat. She was on her second cup of coffee.

He scuffed into the kitchen in his bare feet and said, "Pour one of those for me, will you? What time did you get in?" His once blonde hair was streaked with grey, his blue eyes had lost some of their sparkle, his hands were calloused. Since he lost his wife to cancer five years ago, Ted Crowley's main purpose for living was Amy.

His Ellie's cancer just about devastated the Crowley nest egg, but he was determined to fulfill his promise to his wife....to give Amy the best education that he possibly could. But, it was getting harder.

Amy was fifteen when her mom passed away. She paid attention to every word the doctors said. She began to read medical journals until she understood what was happening to her mother's system. After Ellie died, Amy continued her drive to learn more. What she didn't understand she asked their doctor to explain. Dr. Burns was flattered by Amy's attention to medicine. He was the one who came to her in her senior year and told her about the Romans-Burkas scholarship foundation. She applied and now here she sat with her dad, about to tell him she was indeed one of the winning candidates. She had so much to tell him.

"Did you have a good trip?" he asked as he reached across and took a piece of her toast.

"Dad, I got the scholarship. I start at Harvard in September. If I work hard, and I intend to, I'll end up at Massachusetts General Hospital. I've even been thinking about a specialty, cosmetic surgery. But, I have time for decisions like that. First, I'd like the undergraduate experience of Harvard."

Ted got up and went around the table. He leaned down and kissed her cheek. "I am so proud of you. You deserve this, Amy. You've given up a lot to get the good grades. Your mom is smiling down on you, you know."

She reached up and took his hand, "I know Dad. She's smiling at both of us. You've been working hard, too. There's more I have to tell you."

"What about outside expenses? That's a mighty fine school." His shoulders sagged, he looked worried, his brow was creased.

"Just smile and say you're happy for us. It's a full scholarship in every sense of the word. It covers everything. All the outside expenses will be paid for by the foundation. I tell them what I need and I get it. There's a lot to explain and I need to tell you everything. But first, will you do me a favor and quit your night job at the restaurant? No more two jobs for Amy?"

"But, Amy, I promised your mother…." He started.

"Look," she said as she stood and took his hand. "Look how I got home last night. No cab from the bus station, look." She led him to the living room window and parted the lace curtains.

"I don't understand. Whose car is that?"

"Mine. That's how generous this foundation is. And it will continue to be generous for four years starting in September. I know you like working for Parks and Recreation, that's for you, but nights chopping salads always made me feel guilty. So please quit."

"Your car? Just like that? It's like you won a lottery." His eyes were wide as he stared at the car.

"Let's go down to the Blue Moon and give them your two weeks notice. I'll drive," Amy smiled. "Then we'll go food shopping for a special dinner tonight when I'll tell you all about the people I just met and exactly how this foundation works for me. I'll drive and I'll cook." She was all business.

"We need to thank Dr. Burns," Ted stared at Amy. "Maybe we should invite him to dinner so you can explain all this to him, too."

"No, Dad. This is only between the two of us. We can stop in and tell him I got the scholarship and thank him profusely. All anyone needs to know is that I won a scholarship, period. The details are nobody's business. I go away to school and you get on with your life. You're only 49, handsome and healthy." She poked his shoulder.

Ted reddened and laughed, "Let's go see how that car handles."

Chapter 9

Hal Jensen got to Brownsville, Texas a day before his first class at UT Brownsville. He couldn't wait to finish this semester and get to MIT in September. He had already called his roofer buddy and told him he'd work all summer, but was quitting in September so he could concentrate on school.

His parents were thrilled by Hal's good fortune and relieved to hear that their financial responsibility for him had just come to an end. His brother and two sisters sat around the beat-up living room listening wide-eyed. The girls were twins, the youngest and in the fifth grade. They only understood that Hal had a new car. They were excited to ride in it. Chuck, named after his dad, Charles Jensen, was a junior in high school. He was mostly interested in the application process and how Hal won the scholarship.

"Hard work, my man, high grades, determination and the right priorities," he hit Chuck in the shoulder.

Hal turned to his mom. She was tall, angular and blonde like Hal. She was 45 but looked older. She and Charles both worked in the offices of Hess Oil. They inherited the house from Jean's parents, but even so, they barely made enough to get by. Four growing children kept them as frugal as any couple could be.

Her eyes were wide and brown. Her face was smooth, her cheek bones high. Jean Jensen could be a striking woman. His dad was broad-shouldered, slim waisted, blue-eyed and hair so blonde it was almost white. He had large hands but Hal knew that even though his dad looked like a line-backer, he was the gentlest person in the world.

Jean smiled at Hal, "We are so proud of you Hal. Now I can relax, sure that you will become the engineer you always wanted to be."

Charles sat in the worn recliner. "So, you'll get enough to put you through the year. Then you'll still work summers, is that it?"

Hal hadn't yet told his parents the full extent of the scholarship. He didn't even know why he hadn't. He needed the right moment when he could be alone with the two of them. All of George Ridley's cautions to be discreet were taking root in him. He'd wait until this evening when Chuck was out and the girls were in bed.

"I'll get a stipend plus college expenses will be picked up by the foundation. So you two can now concentrate on Chuck. Don't worry about a college fund for me. I'm going to be just fine." He smiled at them. They stared back at him not quite sure what to say. His mom wiped her hand across her eyes, visibly moved by all Hal had told them.

"It is going to help. But remember, Hal, we are always here for you. MIT is a tough school and there will be expenses you can't even imagine." His dad ran his fingers through his hair. "We will continue to save and even borrow against the house if we have to. We planned to do that anyway."

"You won't have to, Dad. I promise you. You know me. I can live cheap if I have to. He stood to go back to the living room. "Now, I have classes tomorrow so, who wants to go for ice-cream, my treat?"

The twins, Tammy and Terri, heard Hal's last words. They ran to the closet for sweaters. Chuck said, "I ride up front."

As they piled into Hal's new car, Charlie stood on his little front porch. He called to Hal, "You're putting my clunker to shame."

Hal was parked behind Charlie's second-hand Chevrolet station wagon. "It probably rides better than this one. Yours is heavier." He began to back up.

"Bring your mom and me a pint of vanilla."

Hal's sisters oohed and aahed at the plush interior. Chuck put his arm along the top of the seat. "Do you think I could go to college? You know, my grades are not all that bad. Junior year seemed to go pretty well. I had a study partner and that helped me a lot. I'm pulling a lot of B's and next year, I'm taking a pretty easy schedule. But I'll stay with Spanish because my study partner will continue to help me."

"Is this study partner a girl, by any chance?"

"Yeah. But that's all right. She's real smart and helps me a lot, like I said." Chuck was defensive.

"Hey, if it helps, stay with it. Especially if she's cute. Is she?"

"Not bad. Best thing about her is that she's down to earth, know what I mean? But, seriously, could I make it in college? What do you think?"

"Your best bet is to continue to play football. You've played varsity since your freshman year. You're smart, you can think fast. Work with your coach and your guidance counselor. They get scholarship offers on their desks all the time. Let them know you're interested."

Hal sounded older to himself. He wondered if the past week changed him so much.

Chuck was thoughtful, "Wouldn't it be great if we both were on scholarships? I feel sorry for Mom and Dad. All they talk about is money, if they can afford this or that. I'm working this summer, too. I got a job at Wilson's Grocery."

"Good for you Chuck." Hal pulled into the Baskin-Robbins.

"I want a vanilla sundae with sprinkles," squealed Tammy.

Terri laughed out loud, "I'll die if I don't get strawberry, Hal."

Chapter 10

The powder blue baby Buick pulled into the driveway along the right side of the white frame duplex. Marie popped the trunk and took her plaid suitcase to the side door. She was about to unlock it when it was pulled open. Annie Maneras, Marie's grandmother reached for the suitcase. She was a thin, shapeless woman with dark brown curly hair. It looked like a recent home perm. Now it was wet from the shower. Her yellow terry robe was belted tightly and she wore soft white ballet slippers.

"Marie, I expected you yesterday. Did you miss the bus? Let me get the cab fare."

"Gramma, that's not a cab. It's mine," Marie said proudly. "Grandpa, come see my car."

"Don't get him excited, Marie. Let's go inside. Tell us what happened," Annie frowned as she pushed the door shut.

Angelo Maneras was a stocky, balding well-tanned gentleman. He recently had triple by-pass surgery that left him with a slight cough and a long zipper scar down the front of his chest. His cotton robe was unbelted over his pajama bottoms. He hugged Marie warmly.

"What car? What's going on?" Angelo's dark eyes flashed with anticipation. "Is our car all right?"

Marie took him to the window. "Your car is fine. I'm parked right behind you. What do you think? Do you like the color?"

His jaw dropped, "I don't understand."

Annie started to cry softly. "What have you gotten yourself into? You go away for a week and come back with a car? People don't give out cars for nothing unless you got on *Price is Right.*. Did you? Oh, God, I have a bad feeling about this." She put both her hands over her face.

Angelo sat down on the sofa. He looked tired. He sighed, "Because you play the piano someone gave you a car?"

"I won a scholarship because I play the piano well, and because I can write music. Also, my grades were as high as they could possibly be, and because I'm considered an orphan. Also, I got through my freshman year in college. And probably because of a lot of other factors in my screening process that I'll never know about," Marie told them softly.

She shrugged out of her jacket and proceeded to tell them about the full scholarship to Julliard, her plan to work for the summer even though she'd be receiving a stipend during the school year.

Anna and Angelo were postal workers. They worked shifts, the only way they were able to care for Marie. Marie's mother died in childbirth and her father died two years later, from kidney and liver disease. His way of grieving was to drink. After the funeral he'd come by, hold the baby and cry, then leave. Each time he came, he was slurring his speech, crying and whining. Marie's grandparents never even entertained the notion of letting him take the baby. Then his visits became less frequent. When he hadn't come for over a month, Angelo went to his son's apartment and found him unconscious. Two days later he died in the hospital.

They loved their son, but he spun out of control. Someone had to care for the baby. Angelo worked days while Anna became a mother to Marie. Then she went to work three to eleven and Angelo took over. Their routine worked and Marie grew up in a home full of attention and love.

Anna attended school meetings and special events. Marie's best friend in the third grade was Beth Campbell. They took turns having play dates. The first time Marie spent a Saturday afternoon at Beth's house, Helen Campbell let them play at the piano. Marie touched a key and felt magic when the piano responded. Helen, an accomplished pianist, was teaching Beth notes and scales and Marie watched and wanted to try, too. The two girls played together. By the fifth grade, Marie was playing with both hands, she had scales and chords memorized, and could do a fair job with familiar tunes.

In sixth grade, Marie asked for a keyboard for Christmas. She knew that a piano was out of the question not only because of the cost, but also because of the lack of room. Angelo and Annie bought her a Suzuki for sixty-nine dollars. She filled the house with music.

In middle school and high school Marie haunted the music departments. She participated in concerts, was in the school orchestra and never missed a chance to play for events at the school. The priest asked her to play the organ at church when the regular organist couldn't. During her four years at high school she practiced every day on the piano in the school music room and hours at the Campbell's house, hounding Helen to help her with a passage, with her timing, with the pedals. Helen delighted in Marie. She knew in her heart of hearts that Beth would be a good musician for life. She'd enjoy music and teach it to her children. But she knew that Beth's first love was law. Marie, however didn't just enjoy music, she was passionate about it. Helen recognized this and encouraged Marie to experiment, to keep at it. Helen heard of the Romans-Burkas scholarship from her brother who worked in the finance department of Penn State. He told her that Beth should apply. He sent an application to her and Helen noticed a section on need. Beth wouldn't qualify. Not with her husband a judge and she a legal secretary. She did, however, pass the application on to Marie.

Anna was wiping her eyes with a tissue. "You don't need to go back to these people any more do you? Just report to school in the fall and they are all in Chicago, right?"

"Exactly right, Gramma. I am welcome there any time but I don't need to go there. If I have any problems, all I have to do is call George Ridley. He is in charge of our education now. For example, in August, I'll call him to advance me some money to get clothes, a computer, travel expenses and anything else I might need. I'll make a list. I can't ask for jewelry, manicures or anything frivolous, just what I need to make it through my sophomore year at Julliard."

"Phew, Marie, this is so good. About the best thing that's happened since you

came into our lives." Angelo's voice shook. "But I don't like what you said about

being an orphan. We never thought about you that way and we never will. Don't say that again, Marie, please."

"Grampa, I only meant that in the sense of the way I was chosen. Now I want you to do me a favor. Stay on disability, then retire. You have the time in and you're old enough. Why keep on working? A triple by-pass is serious. Now you can relax, travel. Gramma, you're sixty-three. You have thirty years in. Join him. You'll be able to visit me at school. Your pensions and social security will be enough for the two of you to live a comfortable life." Marie held Angelo's hand.

"I can't believe this," said Anna. Grampa and I were just talking about how nice it would be to move to Florida. You know, by Aunt Kate and Uncle Bruno. They love it so much on the gulf."

"I know," Marie said gently. "And they're always asking you to throw away the snow shovel and move by them."

Angelo grew quiet and rubbed his chest. He looked at Marie. "Life dealt you a lousy hand, Maria. We tried to be parents to you, but we always felt that we were falling a bit short. Now, you're wildest dream is coming true. We'll be sad to see you go in September but I guess it's time. You deserve this break so much. Just don't let this scholarship cut you out of our lives."

"Grandpapa, you're my family and always will be. The only family I ever knew. I turned out fine because of you both. I work hard, I study hard, most people like me. I'd say you did a pretty good job." Marie leaned over and hugged Angelo.

Chapter 11

Shirley Carter sat in the overstuffed, threadbare chair. Her feet were up on a round vinyl hassock. Shirley's legs were puffy at the ankles. She wore her shiny black hair in a tight bun. Her smooth caramel colored skin reflected the blue-white light from the television set in front of her. She smiled at the comic on TV. Her teeth were very white and even, one of her blessings. Shirley was plump. She couldn't seem to drop the pounds. She thought it was probably because she ate so much pasta. Pasta was cheap and filling. She also knew that she tasted too many of her own baked goods. Shirley sold her home-made pies, cakes and cookies to two local caterers and one middle school.

Three days a week Shirley worked in the kitchen of the Smithtown Inn. She rose early, at four a.m. By that time she had an oven full of pies. Her own kitchen was big. She had plenty of counter space, her kitchen table took up the center but she longed for another stove. She could get twice as much done if she had another stove.

Frank sat on the sofa cradling a beer. He didn't drink as much as he once did. When they were first married, Frank worked pretty steady as a binder in a carpet factory. Every payday he treated himself to a case of beer. Not that he drank it all at once. It usually lasted almost two weeks.

Then Shirley lost her first and second babies. They were always sad in those days. He also lost his job to a machine. Frank was on unemployment until it ran out. Not a strong man even though he was tall and broad, he was usually tired, couldn't sleep well and lost his appetite a lot.

When Samuel was born, Frank seemed to gain strength from the boy. He took Sam for long walks, pushing the rickety little stroller along the uneven sidewalks of East Smithtown, North Carolina.

"What you got dere, Frank L.?" shouted Rollie the barber. "Come on over here a minit an' show me."

Frank wheeled the stroller across the street to the shop. "My kid, Rollie. My little 'un. Samuel Johnson Carter."

Rollie looked into the stroller, "He's a handsome one, ain't he?"

"Yeah. He's only two months and he sleep through the night," said Frank proudly.

"You not workin?"

"Nah. Collectin'. It be runnin' out soon though. Then I better get the old ass in gear and start lookin' serious, you know?"

"One a the guys comes in here for a cut, talkin' 'bout jobs openin' up in Englewood. Puttin' in one a them Jap car parts factories."

"Prob'ly in that industrial section." Frank adjusted the blanket around Samuel. "Thanks, Rollie. Appreciate it."

"Right. Maybe you could check it out."

Next morning Frank waited until Shirley was ready to deliver her goods to the caterer.

"We're going with you," he said. He held Sam in a blanket.

"What for?"

"Job in Englewood, maybe. Rollie told me to apply. It sounds like something I might like doing. Maybe I could get on second shift if they are going to have one. What do you think?"

"I think I'd like to see a paycheck from you once in a while, mister." She giggled and opened the door for him and Sam.

Frank did get the job. He stocked parts in boxes on metal shelves, and kept a running inventory. He worked three to eleven which was just fine because Shirley was usually finished by noon.

She lost one more baby and told Frank that there would be no more. Dr. Johnson agreed to tie her tubes so she couldn't get pregnant. They both devoted all their attention to Sam. He was a good child, healthy and happy. He grew up curious, obedient and well-mannered. Always a good student, he excelled in both academics and sports. The house was old, but Shirley and Frank made it a home. They worked hard, their health wasn't all that good, but overall they tried to make everything right for Sam.

Frank and Shirley were both forty-four years old. Frank developed high blood pressure and high blood sugar. Dr. Johnson prescribed blood pressure medication and a drug to control his sugar. He started to eat more balanced meals, less fats and he only took small samples of Shirley's desserts.

Now they waited for their son to come home from Chicago. His second semester tuition was in an envelope on the end table in the living room. Twelve hundred dollars twice a year plus his books. It just about wiped out their savings. Well, they were almost finished paying off the loan on Frank's car. *Thank the Lord,* Shirley thought.

"You shouldn't be drinking beer, Frank. No good for you." Shirley sipped her diet soda.

He looked at Shirley for a while. "Know what? It doesn't even taste so good any more, either."

"They have stuff now that gives a man a lot of pep in his step. They advertise it a lot during the soap operas." She raised her eyebrows and smiled wide.

"You are a bad girl, Shirley Carter. A very bad girl." He chuckled low and deep.

They were quiet for a moment.

"What are you thinking?" she asked softly.

He sipped his beer and grimaced. "Well, if he doesn't get this one, there will be others. But, you know, I think they look at black folks last. Just a way of life, I guess. If he never gets a scholarship, we work till we die. I'd like to see him graduate from college, be something professional." He leaned his head back against the recliner.

"We raised him same as whites. We gave him as much as we could afford. We talk the talk in this house. No more we can do, Frankie. No more we can do."

Headlights fanned across the front of the house, tires crunched on the gravel drive. Frank got up slowly. "Must have taken a cab from the station. Big shot."

He parted the lace curtains and peered out the window. Sam was getting out of the car. He went around to the trunk and took out his bag.

"Lordy, lord, lord, Shirley. Step over here. Hurry up." Frank was excited.

Shirley rose slowly and shuffled over to the window. "What are you all goo-goo about now? What am I looking at? What about this car, Frank?" She held her robe tight around her neck.

Sam came in through the kitchen and joined them at the living room window. "No, Dad. I will not be wanting to change cars with you." He laughed deep and loud.

Shirley stared at Sam. "You got it didn't you? You won. I knew you would, baby. We both knew you would. We prayed you would and you did." She hugged him and shook with tears of joy.

"Mamma, why don't you make us a pot of coffee? We need to talk."

They talked and talked. Sam told them about the car and his access money for whatever he needed. He convinced his Mom to call in sick to the Smithtown Inn and to also give them notice to find another kitchen helper. He talked to his Dad about joining the plant credit union and getting in on their stock plan like he always keeps saying he'd like to. They talked about saving and retiring.

Shirley cried a little more. "I don't mind quitting. It would give my legs a rest. And just baking and delivering my cakes and pies would be doing something I enjoy."

"Sam, are you sure about all this? Your education is going to be paid for from now on? Because we can still help you out, you know." Frank was sincere and a little worried.

Sam reached across the kitchen table and patted his father's calloused hand. "It's more than taken care of, Dad. There are even extras that most scholarships don't touch. It's the most generous deal I could ever get. And I will no longer be a financial burden to you two."

Shirley gasped. Her eyes went wide. "Samuel, you have never been any kind of a burden to us. Never. You have been our blessing. And

Frank is right. We are always going to be your backup. You never know what might happen."

Sam heaved a sigh and shook his head. "Promise me you'll not worry about me any more. I'm tired. It's been a weird few days. And I have classes tomorrow afternoon. In the morning I'll drop by the office and pay my tuition."

"The money is in the envelope on the end table," Shirley said.

"That's your money, Mamma. I will be paying my own tuition this term. Then I'll get a job for the summer. Whatever I make will be for you and Dad. I will be paying you room and board until September. Then I'll disappear into the Romans-Burkas Foundation system." Sam grinned.

"Hard to take this all in, son," said Frank. "If you really want to work this summer, maybe you can apply at our brand new loading dock. They added on six new bays and I hear they need some help on the eleven to seven shift. It's all night but it's quiet and you could even study between truck loads."

Sam applied for work at the auto supply parts plant. He was to start May 15 and work until August 30. He went to pay his tuition, then stopped at Sears. He ordered a new stove with an oversized oven. He paid for delivery and installation. Sam had a little money left from the two thousand Ridley gave him. He put that aside for gas. Sam focused on putting this freshman year behind him and heading for UCLA.

Chapter 12

Polio left Frances Kretzler with a pronounced limp. Each step she took with her right foot made her hip jerk out at an impossible angle. She forever wore elasticized slacks a size too large, and loose blouses and sweaters. She sat on the subway and caught her reflection in the window across the aisle. She liked her reddish brown hair pushed up in back with combs. It made the top look puffy and the sides were framed with little corkscrews of stray hairs.

Her partner in medical records at St. Mary's Hospital, fingered Fran's curly hair one day and said, "Why don't you jazz up your hair sometimes, Fran?

She smiled, "How? It just hangs there no matter what."

"Get some combs. Or try a short pony tail. I get bored with mine. That's why I fool with it so much." Jen was a pretty Asian girl with almond eyes and golden skin. Her lips were full and naturally rosy. Fran thought she was a truly beautiful girl. If only her teeth were straight she could be a model. She came to work at records right out of high school. Fran sort of took her under her wing.

"So," Fran kidded, "why don't you get your teeth straightened? You could use a rasp or a round file or something."

They giggled. Jen said, "We better get this pile filed 'fore we get fired. Then I'll never have enough money to get these dumb teeth straight."

"We need a raise, Jen. You should ask Helen to put in for us."

"Maybe in June. Then the half year is up. Think we could get fifty cents an hour more?" Jen was kidding, but she was curious.

Fran thought, "Hmm. The good work we do, and how important they tell us it is all the time, I think we deserve at least a dollar. Imagine, we'd be making ten bucks an hour."

"Yeah, that'd be the day. I could hear business administration now, 'Ten dollars an hour? For sitting down all day putting numbers on papers and filing. No way.' You know that's what they'd say."

They giggled some more.

Jen peered over at Fran over the filing. "Heard from Barry?"

"Not yet. He'll probably be home when I get there. He has classes tomorrow no matter what. He is anxious to finish out his freshman year."

"That was nice of Helen to get you that application for the scholarship," Jen said.

"Yes, it was. She told me that Mr. Romans helped get this hospital going back in the '20's. The clock in the lobby was donated by him in memory of his girlfriend who died here from an infection. The plaque has his name on it. She thought it would be nice if someone with a connection to St. Mary's applied."

"Well, I wish Barry well. He's so smart and he knows what he wants. I finished high school the same year he did and he already has a year of college under his belt. Wish I had that kind of direction." Jen shuffled the papers. "Let's file these and go home. I know you're anxious. Get the four-thirty subway for a change."

Fran stood, stretched and took her folders to the slide out wall of records. She replaced the folders alphabetically.

"See you tomorrow, Jen." Fran took the elevator up to the first floor. She limped down the corridor as fast as she could. She turned left at the clock tower and started to make her way toward the escalator to the subway ramp. She turned back and went to the clock. The bronze plaque said, *Donated by Chet Romans in Memory of Eva Wisinski.*

Fran bent down and touched the plaque. *For luck,* she thought.

The subway lurched to a jolting stop. She rose and made her way up the stairs to the street. She felt apprehensive. Either way, they would get Barry through school. There may be other scholarships to look into, also.

Barry was waiting in the kitchen of their small house, a bungalow, really. Flo and Jack Kretzler bought it when houses were reasonably priced in the upper Broadway section of New York. It was convenient. Jack was a tailor in the men's department at Bloomingdales and Marie worked in the toy department. When Barry was born, she quit to raise him.

After three years in Hebrew school, Barry started the fourth grade in the neighborhood public school. Jack and Fran agreed that she should get some training so that she could get a half decent job when Barry was in school all day. They were both determined to give Barry a fine education. They knew it would cost a lot of money, but they figured they had nine or ten years to add to their savings.

Fran completed a home course on Medical Records and when Barry was in school all day she applied to St. Mary's Hospital. She was hired part time. A year later, she was working five days a week, however, Sunday was one of the days. She loved her job, she did it well. She loved Jack and most of all, she loved her Barry. She showed off his accomplishments whenever she had the chance. His high grades, his science awards, his debating awards.

Jack kept copies of Barry's achievements on the wall of his workshop in Bloomingdales. He was so proud of Barry.

When Barry was in the ninth grade, Jack Kretzler was pushed off the subway ramp into the path of an oncoming train. The train was slowing for the stop, but it was enough to carry Jack fifty feet along the tracks. The resulting broken hip, collar bone, scrapes, internal bleeding and a concussion kept him in the hospital a week before he died.

Barry and Fran stayed with Jack every minute of visiting hours for seven days. Most of the time he was sedated. They each held a hand and talked to him. On the sixth day he opened his eyes and he knew them. His face was mostly bandages but his eyes were open and aware.

He struggled to talk. Barry leaned over and whispered, "Rest, Dad. Don't try to talk. We're here."

Fran kissed her fingertips and put them over Jack's lips. "I love you Jack. Please concentrate on getting better."

His eyes smiled at Fran. "It's almost over here, my love. Take care of our boy. Use the insurance for the savings." His eyes shifted to Barry whose face was wet with tears. "Barry, you're everything to us. Always make the right moves. Make Mom proud. I know you'll always do the right thing."

"Don't talk like this, Dad. Come back to us."

Jack's eyes closed slowly. His hands went limp.

After using most of the thousand dollar insurance money to bury Jack, Fran put the rest into savings and swore she'd find a way to keep her life and Barry's together.

The call from the NYPD came as a surprise to Fran. Two men were arrested for the death of Jack Kretzler and two other victims. Apparently, they picked pockets on the waiting platform and the three times they met resistance, they pushed. They had confessions. They also had Jack's wallet.

"I'm going with you Mom." Barry would not be dissuaded. He talked to the arresting officer. He wanted to know what would happen next. Detective Harrison explained the procedure to Barry. The men were eighteen, but they were seventeen when all this happened. Their parents hired a lawyer to represent the two men. They would be tried as juveniles.

Detective Harrison informed Barry of each step of the process, and when Barry could be present, he was there. It was difficult for him to curb his anger. These boys took so much away from the Kretzlers. He listened to pleas, tried to understand a lawyer who would defend confessed killers, then felt completely defeated when their lawyer won the case for them.

Barry was in the tenth grade when he saw his father's killers go free. He was not muscular. He was thin. His black curly hair made his face look pale.

"Excuse me." Barry stood in front of the two men and their lawyer in the hallway outside the courtroom. One boy was tall and skinny, straight brown hair brushed back, tiny dark eyes. The other was heavy, blocky, soft black hair parted in the middle, pocked skin.

The lawyer looked at Barry. He recognized him from the courtroom. "It's over, son. Take your Mom home now."

"How could you do that?" he asked the lawyer. Then he turned to the two men who killed his father. "I don't know how, but one day you'll have to pay for what you did, and I hope I'm there to see it happen."

They looked at Barry, turned and walked down the corridor to the street. Barry and Flo took the subway home.

"Let it go, Barry," Fran said. "This day is sad enough for us."

"Detective Harrison promised me he'd watch police reports and keep in touch if he came across any contact with Craig Appleby and Jerry Machlich. I have a feeling I may see those two again. New York isn't that big."

Now Barry waited for Fran. He watched her limp down Emerson Street to the front gate and up the short sidewalk to the door. He opened it as she was reaching for her key.

"Surprise," Barry said from behind a bouquet of red roses. He shifted them aside and grinned at her.

"You got the scholarship?" Her eyes went wide. "I need to sit down." She hugged him and flopped onto the sofa. "Barry, tell me all about it. God, I'm ecstatic. Wait till I tell Jen and my supervisor. What a great thing this is, Barry," she sobbed quietly. "I wish your father could be here to know this, to feel this joy. I'm babbling. Tell me about your week in Chicago."

"Mom, I have so much to tell you. The scholarship is for four years so I can go to graduate school after I finish my three years. Isn't that great? The scholarship covers the three years I need to finish my undergraduate degree, then I have another year left on it to get a masters. This fall I'll be starting my sophomore year....are you ready for this? At Harvard."

Fran gasped. "They'll pay for Harvard?"

"All expenses, too. I'll receive a stipend to cover anything that may come up during the year. I wish you could meet these people on the Foundation board. They are spectacular. I don't know exactly how they chose us, but we are a great mix of students and as a board, they are the most sincere, supportive people I ever met, except you, of course."

"My God, Barry. It sounds too good to be true. But what did you mean by 'we are a great mix of students'?"

He took off his jacket and loosened his collar. "There were five finalists and at first I thought we were in a final interview. I was sure the board was going to pick only one of us. We were all so nervous and almost sick with tension. Then we were told that all five of us would be getting the scholarship."

"So you're all paid up for the coming year?" she asked tentatively.

"The next four, Mom. Get used to it. The money you make at the hospital is yours. I'll work this summer as a grunt in some law office for the experience, but no more money worries, okay?" He smiled. "By the way, did you notice the white Buick parked on the street in front of the house?"

"No, why?" Fran looked puzzled.

"It's mine. The foundation felt it would be helpful if we had cars. What do you think?" He led her to the front window.

"We never had a car. I don't know what to say."

"Get used to some luxury in our lives, Mom. We are going to relax and enjoy life a little bit now. I start classes tomorrow. I'll take you to work in the morning, pick you up at the end of the day and we'll go to Percy's for dinner. My treat. Let's start to feel good about all this, okay?"

Her eyes welled up once again. "We haven't been to Percy's for years."

"I know. It's time."

Chapter 13

George Ridley called them all on the twelfth of August to tell them that Jim Randal passed away. There was to be a memorial service on the fifteenth. He was requesting their presence at the service. Airline tickets would be waiting for them at their nearest airport. They would be picked up at O'Hare and driven to Bluff View. They all agreed to attend.

The Randals were Episcopalians. The service was stunning. There were flowers, candles, music, especially the music. Muriel Karetsky sang "Amazing Grace" a capella. There wasn't a dry eye in the church. Her voice filled every marble and mahogany nook in the church. In her late sixties and she still sang like crystal. When she was finished she sat next to her children, Edward Vincent and Lisa.

The service was foreign to Sam who was raised Baptist and Barry, who was Jewish, but they felt the power and beauty of it and were impressed.

Afterwards, at the Romans' house, the five met with Ridley and started to tell him what they thought they needed to properly begin their sophomore year.

He held up his hand, "There won't be any need for that this year. Jim Randal mentioned all of you in his will. 'To all candidates who attend my funeral, I bequeath the sum of twenty-thousand dollars in cash with no restrictions, totally unrelated to the Romans-Burkas Foundation.'

So, here you go." He handed them each bulky manilla envelopes. "I know it's unrelated, but you have the opportunity to leave this year's fifty-thousand ride."

"It's more than enough," Hal said. "As a matter of fact, let me give you ten to put in my account. I made over two thousand doing roofing jobs this summer."

"They each decided that ten would be more than they were planning to request from Ridley.

George put all their money in his briefcase, pulled out their folders and made a note on each one indicating a deposit of eight-thousand dollars.

"Now you each have fifty-eight thousand dollars in your accounts. I'll get statements out to you monthly because with investments, your accounts will be changing."

They looked at each other and smiled.

Sam said, "I forgot about your four percent, George. Man, I just spent my whole summer's earnings in the blink of an eye. For a moment, I thought I had sixty." He chuckled.

"Trust me. We'll get you to sixty sooner than you think. Always remember, dealing with Ridley Associates is a win-win deal."

They shook hands all around. George left. Amy made a pot of coffee. "Let's relax before we head over to the Randals."

Hal tugged at his jacket. "Do we have to dress formally to visit the Randals? I need to get out of this suit and tie." He disappeared upstairs followed by Sam and Barry. The girls had their coffees on the sun porch.

"All set for Julliard, Marie?"

Marie gazed out at the lake, the boats, the neat docks. "I'm scared to death, Amy. I've never been away from home more than a one-night sleepover at a girlfriend's house."

"Me too. I really hate leaving my Dad all alone. He has been both mother and father to me for so many years, that I'm afraid when he's left alone, he's going to short circuit."

"Do you ever feel that this is like a dream? That any moment someone is going to come to you and say it's all been a terrible mistake?"

Sam stood in the doorway in grey sweats and a navy pullover. His sneakers were brand new white. "Yes, Marie. I feel it too. But it's no mistake. I look over my shoulder every day looking for a man in a suit carrying a folder with someone else's name on it. And he'll tell me that it wasn't me, but this other fellow, whose name is on the folder, he's the one who was chosen, not me, not Sam Carter. But we can't give in to those ideas. This is real. What Jim Randal just did is real. This can't be a mistake. We were thrown a pass and now we have to run with it the best way we can. We have to make these folks proud of their investment in us."

The girls looked him over. Marie said with a smile, "Hey, look at you. You look like you're ready to go out on that *Eva* boat."

He struck a pose. "Master of my ship. Care to take a spin?"

Hal came into the sunporch. He had changed into khaki slacks, loafers and a red polo with a Nike logo. His hair was damp and curly.

"Not without me. Let's go for a ride and catch the sunset over the lake. Hey Barry, hurry it up," Hal shouted up the steps.

Barry came down in his suit. "What's going on? I was on the phone with my mother."

Hal pointed up the steps. "You have five minutes to get casual, pal. Then we're weighing anchor without you, you hear?"

They all went to the dock and undid the ropes, hoisted the anchor and prepared to shove off the dock. Barry came running along the wooden dock. He had shorts and a long-sleeved sweater on. He was waving his white cap. "Wait for me."

He jumped from the dock and landed on the moving deck of the *Eva,* sprawled at Sam's feet. He looked up and said, "I'm glad I made it."

Sam looked down at Barry and said, "This boat was just coming in, suh."

They broke into gales of laughter. Hal shoved the boat away from the dock. Amy started the engine. Hal steered them away from the dock and out to sea.

Ada sat on Muriel's deck. Muriel had tea for them set out on the wicker table. She said to Muriel, "Who's taking out the *Eva?*"

Muriel squinted at the boat and smiled. "It looks like our five students are going to try their hands at boating."

"I hope they know what they're doing." Ada sipped her tea.

Marie sat on the cushioned bench and held on to the rail. "I hope I don't get sick. I've never been out on a boat before."

Sam sat next to her. "I'm not exactly one of the yachting crowd, either. You want a soda? There's a cooler up front."

"Maybe that would help."

Sam rose and started to move forward when Hal turned sharply to head out to deeper water. Sam lost his balance and was thrown against the rail. He flipped over and fell head first into the cold water. Amy ran to the bench, stepped up and dove into the water. Barry grabbed the *Eva* life preserver. Marie, Hal and Barry pulled with all their might to get Sam, then Amy back aboard.

Hal got two blankets out of the first aid box. "Get out of your clothes and into the blankets," Hal shouted.

Sam sputtered, "Damn, that happened too fast."

Amy was beside him. "You need to get your sea legs working. I'll show you how."

They both sat huddled in their blankets, sipping sodas.

"Thank God it's July," Barry laughed. "We'll string your clothes up and they'll be dry in about forty five minutes."

"Ada, these were the brightest of the bright, correct?" Muriel took a sip of her tea and nodded at the scene out on the *Eva*. "Someone should tell them it's dangerous to swim with their clothes on."

"They are bright kids, Muriel. I'm sure they know what they're doing." Ada picked up a scone and took a bite. "Remember how we used to go on outings on the boat? We swam and fished and tanned ourselves."

Muriel sighed. "I miss those days, Ada. That they ever ended is still a surprise to me."

"Yes, a sad surprise. I feel I need to do something to keep my life going. You have your grand kids. I have no one. I get lonely sometimes. Kate and I are planning some trips abroad. The islands, maybe even Australia."

"I'm having some fun watching the grand kids grow. They give me so much pleasure. I'm lucky that they live close enough to spend as much time with me as they do. I miss my Jozef, though. I wish he could be part of their lives."

"Do you ever think of Pete and Chet?" Ada buttered a second roll. "You know, Pete probably loved me more than I loved him, but I grew to admire him over the years. His life was tough, he was tough, but he enjoyed what he did because he was handicapped and was able to hold his own. He brought Chet out here to Chicago, you know. And they both pulled Carlie into the carting business. If it wasn't for those three guys, I wouldn't be sitting here today planning exotic trips and laughing at five youngsters I'm going to help put through college."

"I know, Ada. And Chet brought me to the Karetskys where I learned how to cook and fall in love with Jozef. If it wasn't for Chet and Pete, I wonder where we'd be? Not on the North Shore, I bet." Muriel gazed at the sun-washed water. She started to chuckle. "Look. They have their wet clothes strung around the boat. They must have fallen overboard. We'll have to get the story when they get back."

Chapter 14

The five of them pounded up the stairs to the deck of the Romans' house. Jan Harcher and her son, Brian met them on the top. They were all laughing.

Jan threw her shiny hair back and smiled. "Who fell overboard?"

Sam put his palm to his chest, "Guilty. I lost my footing. You should have seen Amy. She dove right in and saved my hide."

Amy blushed. "I swim a lot in Lake Erie. My dad takes me fishing with him once in a while. He fishes, I swim. I just reacted."

"We kind of thought you weren't just taking a dip when we saw your clothes waving in the wind," Jan giggled. "I'd like you all to meet my son, Brian Harcher." She turned to Brian and took his arm. "He's visiting from California. He was on his way here when Mr. Randal passed away."

She introduced the five to Brian. They shook hands. Marie said, "Let us change then I'll make a pot of coffee and we can talk."

Jan agreed. "Go ahead and change. Brian and I know our way around Chet's house."

Jan and Brian went into the kitchen and set out plates and cups. The coffee maker was brewing and Brian took a white paper bag with the Lakeside Inn logo on the side from the counter. He placed pastries on the large platter.

Hal came down the stairs into the kitchen, his hair damp. "Looks good enough to eat," he said.

Marie and Amy squealed in delight at the Karetsky goodies. They all sat around the table munching on tarts and filled pastries.

"I'm going to drive to Chicago every chance I get just to eat at the Lakeside," said Barry sipping his coffee.

Jan smiled, "The foundation board wants you to use this house like it's your own. Visit whenever you feel the urge….vacations, special occasions, just relax when you have the time. We really want to get to know you and we want to enjoy your progress. That was what the two founders were all about. Pete and Chet loved to watch what money could do for people."

"That's great. I'd love to bring my folks here to enjoy the beach, the boat, the food. My mom would love all this baked stuff. She bakes in town and sells her goodies to a school, a caterer, whoever wants to buy." Sam shook his head. "I think about this all the time and wonder how I got so lucky."

Marie laughed. "My grandparents are so suspicious. They need to meet the board just to put their minds at ease. They're nervous wrecks until I get home safely."

Hal sat up straight, "Why not come for spring break?"

Brian said, "I'm glad you didn't say Christmas vacation. We get a ton of snow and ice here in December."

Jan nodded, "Spring break would be better. You won't have room here for everybody, but some of you can stay with Muriel and Ada, and me. The Harchers would also put up a few. We all have big houses with plenty of room. Let's make it a definite date then."

They ate all the pastries, had second cups of coffee and Jan said she had to run to the TV station for the ten p.m. news. The said they'd be sure to watch.

Brian remained with the five. He talked about his work with computers in Silicon Valley.

"What do they do, exactly?" Barry wanted to know. "My Mom said they're going to be getting them at the hospital to help keep records."

"That's one application, Barry. Right now the biggest attraction is games. They're real hot. The big money is in creating programs that design games. Like Star Wars, Pac Man, all the Nintendo stuff."

"Is that what you do?" asked Hal.

"I'm working on the micro-chips that go inside the unit. It's so fascinating. It's a new language, a new challenge every day. It's like getting in a fast car and speeding down highways of ideas that are all interconnected by the chips. The company I work for is making great strides in miniaturizing the whole package. The first computers were as huge as this room. Now they fit on top of a desk. Soon we'll be able to carry them around with us wherever we go."

Sam was skeptical. "I hear they are very expensive. Too expensive just to play games."

"Well, as Barry just said, the hospitals will keep their records stored on computers instead a hundred file cabinets. Schools will use them to keep track of grades and attendance. Some police stations have systems installed to keep track of crimes in their precincts. The applications for all types of businesses are endless." Brian sounded passionate.

"You really love what you do, don't you? Where did you study, Brian?" asked Amy.

I started at the Wharton School of Finance. When I finished, my dad took me to California. He had a pal who worked at Canyon Computers. With my finance training, they offered me a position in their business office. That was my first experience with computers and the people who use them."

"Must have been scary," said Sam.

"Yeah, it was. But computer people are an entire breed of their own. Two guys from the department spent hours with me every day for a week. They stayed until midnight getting me to be comfortable with all the buttons, all the things it could do."

"It must have worked. You sound like you're really into it now." Marie sipped the last of her coffee. "It sounds so technical, so complicated."

"Marie, it's my life. Now you're all going to start school next month. I need a favor. I want to give you each an experimental computer. It's set with some programs I'm hoping you'll find helpful. Will you use it for a year then let me know what you think? Sort of critique it as a tool?" Brian looked at them questioningly.

"I'm game," said Amy. They all agreed.

"Then I need the name of the college you'll be attending so I can get these to you at the start of the year." He handed them his card. "Call me when you have a dorm address, or apartment, or wherever you'll be in September. I'll arrange to get these to you." Brian got up to leave.

"How did your mom meet Chet Romans?" Barry asked.

"We all have stories around here," Brian laughed. "Ours is simple. Chet put a note in an old armoire about calling Ridley. Whoever found the note was asked to go to Chicago and talk to him. We lived in Indiana, found the armoire at a flea market and I broke a drawer, but found the note. The rest, as they say, is history."

"So your mom and you relocated, and he gave her some money?"

"Yes, Barry. She got the education in communications that she always wanted, met and married Kevin, I got a dad, my Grandma Judy sold her house and came to live with us.

Kevin and my mom built a great house. It would have been happily ever after if my dad didn't get killed on an assignment. Now my grandmother, Mom and I are still together, but Kevin Harcher left an empty space in our lives."

"I remember when he died. It was on the news for a whole week. Nice looking man. What a shame," Amy said sincerely.

There was a moment of awkward silence. Then Brian headed for the door. "Remember," he said. "I want to hear from you. Comments, problems, anything. Okay?" Brian looked all excited. The computer illiterates merely shook their heads, unsure of what they would ever do with a computer.

Chapter 15

Over the course of the first scholarship year, the five faithfully kept in touch with the board. Some of them hounded Brian. Marie discovered a program that enabled her to compose and save musical transcriptions. Hal insisted that Brian and his company work on developing programs that tested tensile strength of metals, metal fatigue, soil composition and analysis of core samples. Sam, at UCLA was looking into post graduate work in orthopedics. He used the computer for record keeping, but was getting seriously interested in all the new medical machinery. He asked Brian to look into somehow incorporating computers and medical testing for faster and more accurate results. Barry admitted that he used his to write reports for classes and a little record keeping. Amy, too, couldn't see much value in the computer except for homework assignments and keeping her schedule straight. They all agreed that they saw computers, with the right applications, as a useful tool in the future.

Brian took their suggestions, thanked them and told them to keep the computers and to call him with any other applications they could think of.

"I've created monsters," Brian told his boss. "But some of this we can run with. That business of incorporating medical machinery with the computer is particularly challenging."

The board was pleased when they got copies of their transcripts. All five ended the sophomore year with solid four point grade averages, the highest. They had adjusted well to college life. All five continued their summer jobs. Barry, however, left the small law firm he had been with and went to work in the city court house, in the records department.

Chapter 16

Near the end of the summer, the five received health insurance cards from Liberty Insurance of Chicago. After reading the accompanying letter, they realized that not only were they insured, but their families as well. There were two cards in each envelope, one for them and one for the family. Sam Carter thought about his folks and how they couldn't afford doctors. The insurance covered office visits, hospital care and pharmaceuticals. Barry Kretzler couldn't wait to give his mom the card. Marie thought the insurance was as good as the scholarship. It opened the medical care door to her grandparents.

Ted Crowley looked at the blue and yellow insurance card. He sat at the kitchen table and held it by its edges in his two hands. He was fifty years old, in good health and thanks to Amy's foundation, he was worry free for the first time since his Ellie passed away.

"Well, I'm pretty healthy, Amy. But like the card says, it is insurance."

"I hope you never need to use it, Dad. But the initial check-up would be a good idea. Complete blood work, urinalysis, heart, lungs, the works."

"Yes, Dr. Amy. These people in Chicago sure know how to sweep away the problems, don't they?" Ted smiled warmly at Amy as she worked in the kitchen. She was baking a lasagna and tossing a salad for their dinner.

"You know, Dad, this scholarship is for five years. But I think I can get my junior and senior years condensed into one. Then I'll go to Mass. General School of Medicine. I'm sure I'll be able to squeeze those first two years into one. Then I can begin my internship."

"Amy, I need to talk to you. Everything is falling into place nicely for you now. We are both relaxed, no tension, because you, Miss Smarty have erased our money worries."

"So?" She threw a leaf of lettuce at him. He caught it and chewed on it. "Well, you're away a lot now. I poke around here trying to keep up with the old house. My highlight is going shopping to the grocery store."

"Let's go to Bluff View for a few days. We can go fishing. The house and boat is always available to us." She set the table slowly. "Is it something else?"

"Yes, Amy. Now hear me out, please…."

"This sounds like a woman. Is it? Really? I don't believe it." Her eyes were wide, glassy.

"Let me tell you what happened," he began.

Amy dropped the utensils on the table with a crash. She grabbed her purse off the chair by the door and left quickly.

Ted put his head in his hands. "Ellie, Ellie, I'm so sorry. What can I do?"

Amy drove three blocks to a small playground. She parked the car and walked to one of the swing sets. She sat and gently pushed herself back and forth. She kept her head down and let herself sob for her beautiful mother.

She went over to the water fountain and splashed cold water over her face. She rose up and pushed her hair back behind her ears. Two little pigtailed girls were waiting to use the fountain.

"Why are you washing your face?" the taller of the two asked.

"She was crying," whispered the little one.

Amy smiled, "I had something in my eye. You need help getting a drink?" She squirted the water high. The two girls giggled as they took turns catching the cascading water into their open mouths.

"Are you two sisters?" asked Amy.

"No," said the older girl, "but we are best friends."

The two very soaked girls ran to the see-saw. The older girl put the smaller one on and proceeded to give her a gentle ride up and down.

Amy watched them for a while. They were lucky to have each other Amy knew.

She returned to the kitchen. It was empty. She continued to set the table. Ted came into the kitchen and watched her.

"So, when am I going to meet your friend?" Her voice was calm, even.

"Amy, I know that families split apart over things like this, but...."

"You are alone too much, I agree. My reaction was a selfish one. But I couldn't help it." She took the lasagna out of the oven, "It's just that I can't imagine anyone with you in this house except Mom."

"That's another thing, Honey. I'm going to sell this house and move in with Ceil. God, this is so hard for me. I don't want to hurt you, but, I've made some plans and I'm pretty excited about the changes."

"Ceil? Ceil Resko?" Amy began to pace. "Is that who you're talking about?"

"Amy, I need for us to sit and talk. Please don't turn me off again."

Amy seemed defeated. She smiled tiredly. "No, Dad, I'm not going to be unreasonable. I can almost see how this happened. Ceil and Mom were friends. She turned to both of you when Mr. Resko passed away. You traveled around together. Then when Mom passed away, she was supportive. Then, I guess one thing led to another...."

Ted sat at the table. "Amy, please don't be bitter. I need you to be okay with this. What you just said is pretty much it. It simply happened. We both suffered tremendous loss and we turned to each other. She started to come over with food, she brought pictures of trips the four of us were on over the years. We shared stories. It was so much relief. I was finally able to talk about Ellie and smile about things we did. It just felt right."

"I'm sorry you couldn't talk to me. I'm so wrapped up in myself, I forget about what you must be going through. I'm not so smart after all, am I?"

"You're doing exactly what you should be doing. Your mom and I are very proud of you. It was your intelligence, after all, that got you on the right track. I'm sure she's looking down on you and cheering you on. Please, don't let me be an obstacle for you. I couldn't live with that."

She sat across from him and reached over to put her hand over his. "The only reason I got that scholarship is because you and Mom did so much for me up until the day I applied. Remember the tutors, the trips, the special books, anything I needed to get the high grades? That's how I felt I was qualified to apply. It was because of you both."

"She loved you as I love you. You're important to us. Like all parents, we wanted to give you all that we could."

"And now I'm acting like a selfish brat. I'm out there meeting new people and making new friends all the time. Who am I to deny you the same? You must think I'm a real jerk."

"No, no, I understand. If I were in your shoes, I'd probably react the same way. But we will never give up the memories of your mom, never."

"I know. So the lasagna is cold. Let's go out for some supper, okay? I'll put this all in the fridge for tomorrow."

He smiled at her and mouthed, "Thank you."

Chapter 17

Ceil Resko lived in a quiet neighborhood on a cul-de-sac, first house on the right as the circle began. It was brick and pale yellow clapboard. The front garden was well-tended, roses under the bay window and marigolds lining the sidewalk. Amy knew the house. She had been here many times to celebrate birthdays, or just a Sunday dinner.

They stood on the front porch, Amy holding the half of a cherry cheesecake they bought at the restaurant before they left. Ted tapped on the door. He was visibly tense.

Ceil opened the door and smiled. "Ted, Amy, what a nice surprise. Come on in." Ceil did not look forty eight. Her hair was a soft black and layered along her face to just below her ears. She wore a grey sweat suit with white sneakers. She was attractive in a relaxed, homey way. She had wide brown eyes, a dazzling smile and smooth, almost olive skin. Amy compared her to her mother and to Amy, Ellie was different, a natural beauty who didn't need makeup, or a dye job. But Amy realized she was being unfair.

She handed the box to Ceil and pecked her on the cheek, "Good to see you, Mrs. Resko."

"Please, Amy, call me Ceil, okay?"

"Just don't expect me to call you Mom," Amy reddened. She was sorry the moment she said it.

Ceil's eyes teared. "There's no reason for that, Amy. I knew Ellie

69

long before she was married. You were her life. I know how she loved you. And you and your dad loved her."

"Damn. I'm sorry. I really am. It's just that I'm accepting all this, but a part of me still can't. But I promise you, I'm not going to be a problem. I hate feeling like a spoiled little kid." She hugged Ceil.

Ted went into the kitchen and started a pot of coffee. He put out some plates and forks, spoons and began to slice the cheesecake. Amy noticed that he looked comfortable, like he belongs here. Ceil's kitchen was large with cabinets lining three walls, counters underneath. They sat at the round table in the center.

"Your garden looks pretty," Amy said.

"I don't spend as much time in it as I used to. I plant a lot of seeds in the spring and they take care of themselves. I'm pretty busy these days trying to keep up with office work." Ceil worked as an executive secretary for a large insurance firm in downtown Erie. "My boss wants me to learn to keep records on a computer and it's driving me nuts. There are four of us at Crusader Mutual struggling with Apple PC's."

"I have a computer at school. I use it for keeping assignment dates, writing homework papers and researching latest medical techniques and trends."

"Does it ever, like, freeze up for you? You know, stall out? I never know what to do. I feel so helpless."

"I know a man in California, Brian Harcher," Amy wrote Brian's name and number on the cheesecake box. "Call him from work and tell him exactly how your computer is acting. He'll walk you through the program and tell you how to get it back on track. He's a whiz."

Ceil put the box on the counter. "I will, Amy. I need all the help I can get. "

They wandered out to the deck. Amy told Ceil that the garden looked Victorian with all the flowers in bloom. The colors were vibrant. Butterflies and finches flitted among the blooms. Amy walked down the steps to the brick path. She sat on a wooden bench surrounded by zinnias and cosmos. Ceil joined her. Her black hair gently caught the light breezes.

Amy turned to Ceil and took her hand. "Ceil, please believe me when I say this is hard for me. But seeing my dad here with you, well, it's somehow right for him. If he needs someone, I'm happy it's you. I mean that sincerely." Tears streaked her face.

Ceil leaned over and hugged her. "Oh, Amy. I would never dishonor your mother's memory. I loved her, too, you know. We were friends for so many years. When Paul died your parents helped me through that grief. Then when Ellie died, your dad turned to me. It helped both of us to share the memories of our mates. It really does help to sit and talk. Then we began to go to places the four of us traveled to in the old days. We went to movies, plays, retirement workshops, dinners...."

"I know. These things happen. You don't have to explain. You and Dad should be together. I really am happy for you both, Ceil. Dad is so relaxed around you because he has known you for so long, he's comfortable. God, I should be thanking you."

She leaned over and picked a pink zinnia. She handed it to Amy. "Ted and I are like two best friends. Be friends with us. That's all I ask."

Amy gazed at the garden. There was a little fountain bubbling near the bird bath. She thought of the two little friends in the playground. She poked the zinnia in her hair and smiled at Ceil.

Chapter 18

Chad Fergis drove the four wheeler through the dense pine forest. The dirt logging road was rutted from the constant heavy truck traffic. He needed to check with the foreman before he left on his trip to Washington.

"Hey, Chad," Rusty called from the top of a log cutting machine. He jumped down and walked over to Chad. "When you leavin'?"

"Early tomorrow morning, Rusty. Everything okay out here?"

"Yeah." Rusty spit into the pine debris. "Should get out at least six truckloads today. When is Northern takin' over?"

"I signed the papers yesterday. It'll take them five years to finish with me, though. In the meantime, you have any gripes, you go to Walt Harris. He's going to listen to anything you have to say, Rusty. I've known him for years. He's regular. He'll be able to contact me." Chad reached into his shirt pocket and handed Rusty a piece of paper. "Here's his number at Northern Evergreen's office. Rusty, they want everything to be the same. We been dealin' with them since my grandpa had the business."

"I know, Chad. They were always our biggest customer. Just seems funny not workin' for you any more. Gene Fergis Logging just won't be the same. But, you need to do what you think is right for you. You keepin' the house?"

"For now. Here's the key in case there are any problems. Use the office in the back for yourself until they kick you out. Guess it'll be pretty wide open for the next few years." Chad sounded excited. "Tell the others for me that I've arranged a little bonus for all fourteen of you in the next paycheck."

"I'll tell 'em. I'm almost jealous, pal. But I think I'd be like a fish out of water if I was to leave the woods." He laughed phlegmy chuckle. "Nice send-off party, wasn't it?"

"You bet, Rusty. Nice watch. I really appreciate it." There was an uncomfortable silence among the massive pines. Off in the distance the heavy log cutters were at work. Their insistent drone pierced the stillness.

"I'm not going to China, Rusty. I'll be back visiting before too long."

The sun was just coming up over the low hills around the old log house Chad's father had built when Chad was a tot. Chad loaded his two large suitcases into the back of his Jimmy. He closed the door and slowly pulled down the long driveway to the gate onto the logging road that would take him to the first paved back road that eventually found a four lane to the end of Maine. He was already planning a return trip next year. Damn, he thought. I'm lonesome already. He laughed out loud as he bounced along the rutted road sending up a steady wake of yellow dust.

He leaned out the window and shouted into the pines, "See you next year, Elk Pond."

Half way through New York State he pulled into a Marriot, had some supper and slept all night. After breakfast he walked around the hotel grounds, the pool area and the truck depot on the adjacent lot. He took in all the noise, the constant movement of the 18 wheelers and wondered if he'd ever miss the north woods..

He headed back to the highway ramp smiling to himself. He thought about Rosie dumping him. Cute, cuddly Rosie. But they were going nowhere. Too many dates, lots of loving, but no commitment on either side. Chad wondered what their relationship was all about. He felt secretly relieved that Rosie was now a part of his past.

Chapter 19

The red brick buildings seemed to be pushed together arbitrarily, like children's blocks, some high, some squat, some even askew. Inside, the halls were a maze of departments, wards, units, areas and zones. Massachusetts General Hospital, a symphony of confusion, disjointed like a jazz concert but to Amy Crowley, intern, it was a challenge that she met head on. She loved the change of assignments from pediatrics to geriatrics, the labs, oncology and on and on in her march to becoming a certified internal medicine specialist. Next on her assignment list was emergency medicine. She spent half the night studying trauma, burns, triage, various ways the human body ended up pierced, invaded and smashed.

She turned the corner into the hallway that would take her to the emergency room.

She looked at his face as he neared her. She frowned. "Barry?"

Barry Kretzler, Harvard law, raised his eyebrows and smiled in surprise.

"Hello there, Amy. It's been a while. What's going on?" He seemed taller to Amy, more confident, much more mature.

"Is anything wrong? Are you okay?" She reached out her hand and they shook warmly.

"My mom. She's having a hip replacement operation. Her doctors in New York sent her here because she's going to need some work done on back realignment, too. Convenient for me since I'm right next door at Harvard Law. Do you realize that we've been here almost four years and this is just the second time I've seen you?"

"Bummer, isn't it? I have about an hour before I go on duty. Got time for a coffee?" Amy took his elbow. "I do know where the cafeteria is."

"That's fine. We can catch up a little."

Over coffee they compared notes about all the condensing of classes and testing processes to gain exemptions and move ahead faster.

Amy sipped her decaf. "I suppose we're both in a hurry to get where we're going, right?"

Barry nodded, "I want to be a part of the New York District Attorney's team so badly, Amy. I follow all their cases, the way they're handled, the outcomes. It's the most exciting place I know and I'm driven to become a part of it." He blushed at Amy. "I guess I sound kind of dorky, eh?"

"No way. I was just thinking of how much we both have changed since that day in Ridley's office.

"I guess when an event like that happens to you, change is inevitable. I've been on a roller coaster ride since then. Being at Harvard is incredible even though I spend about eighteen hours a day reading law, with no let up. It's addictive to me. I research cases on the computer. I'm in constant contact with Brian Harcher. He sends me current case file programs. Then my mom. She fell and injured her hip. If not for our great insurance she'd never be getting all this wonderful work done on her. You met her, remember? At Bluff View."

"Of course. She was born with polio and an uneven back alignment. She told me all about it. She has a good attitude, as I remember."

"Mom's always been upbeat. She ended up at St. Mary's as a patient because she worked there for years. Now she's going to walk straight..." his voice dropped.

Amy reached across the table and took his hand, "We have the best team of neurosurgeons in the country right here. Of course she's going to walk normally after they work their magic on her." She sounded so sincere.

Barry looked uncomfortable. "It's not that. I'm confident in the doctors. She has a gentleman friend. A man from our temple. Very nice. He's good to her. They'll probably marry one day. I'm struggling with it, but she is over fifty." He shrugged his shoulders.

Amy put her hand over his, "Welcome to the club. My dad is lately involved as well."

"Oy. Think it's something in the water?" Barry's face relaxed, his eyes crinkled.

"If it's the water, I better hit the well," she giggled.

"Where would you ever get the time for a relationship? You're like me. Love would be just another thing to do."

She sighed. "You're right, Barry. Time is of the essence for people like us. But, there'll come a day, eh?" She bent her head toward him, then glanced at her watch. "I have to go. ER awaits. But let's plan a get together. Coffee?"

"Hasty Pudding? They serve a pretty nice crepe."

"Yuck. I ate there once. I had lamb that was like shoe leather. Do you know that diner on Saugus? The one that's open all the time?"

"Sure. City Diner. I often grab a breakfast there around 5 a.m."

Amy thought for a moment. "Today is Thursday. See you there Sunday at five, okay?"

He got up and took her arm. "Is that a date, doctor?"

"You bet, Barry. It's a date."

Chapter 20

The wipers beat a steady slap-slap on the windshield as Chad noticed the traffic increasing. It was two-thirty p.m., not exactly rush hour, but the ramp exits and entrances were becoming more frequent, and more crowded. He clicked into the middle lane to avoid merging cars that never slowed down but depended on the interstate traffic to let them merge in, room or not. He was using his mirrors more now as speeding cars and trucks passed him on both sides and hung on his tail.

He was a bit uncertain as he looked for the by-pass around Boston. He was hoping it wouldn't be too long before it eventually re-connected to the interstate. Up ahead he saw the sign over the road. He put his right signal on and began to drift over. The car ahead of him was changing lanes at the same time. Chad hit his brakes to slow down. The tanker truck driver cursed as he swerved to avoid the GMC. He hit Chad's left back bumper sending him careening onto the shoulder, catching the exit number sign, and flipping over the embankment next to the ramp.

The trucker radioed for help, ran down to the overturned car and frantically tried to get Chad out of the smoking wreckage. Three men slid down the grass and rushed over to help. One man had a tire iron. He broke the driver's side window. The trucker reached in and released the seat belt. Chad, bleeding and unconscious, slumped onto the inside roof of the upturned vehicle. They quickly pulled him out onto the grass.

"Get him away from the car," shouted a young man rushing down the hill. He had a seat cushion in his hand. He positioned it around Chad's head and secured it with the arms of a sweater.

"I called Mass Gen. I'm an EMT there. They're going to send a helicopter." He had them lift Chad gently, but quickly, back away from the car which was smoking more and more. Sirens sounded in the distance as police and fire

trucks rushed to the scene.

Traffic was stopped, hoses were aimed at the car. It exploded into a fireball. The white chemical from the fire hoses spread over the car creating a black column that drifted up into the afternoon sky. Chad missed it all.

Chapter 21

Amy felt so much better after her talk with Barry. She appreciated what her father was feeling. Somehow, knowing that Barry had the same misgivings about his parent helped her to see hers in a more sensible light. She also felt a little lonely when Barry left her to visit his mother.

The ER was a frantic place. Patients needed help immediately, snap judgments had to be made, applications administered to wounds, urgent orders shouted at nurses and interns. No time to think, just to act.

A harried doctor faced her, lifted her name tag and said, "Dr. Crowley, get to the entrance stat. We have an auto accident victim. Male, head injury."

That's all. And she ran. She met the gurney outside. The EMT shouted, "Multiple fractures, head injury, possible internal bleeding."

She helped push the gurney down the hall. "Last cubicle on the right," she said as she helped to swing the back end out and pushed the front into the room. Chad was quickly lifted and placed onto the bed.

All of Amy's skills were forced into play. She stopped external bleeding, cleaned and bandaged open cuts, examined for broken bones. One leg was fractured, a collar bone was popped out. She tracked down the doctor with the preliminaries.

"He may have internal bleeding. There's head trauma. I suggest an MRI and some X-rays."

"Do it Dr. Crowley." He signed her patient sheet.

"Orderly," she called as she began to push the gurney back out into the hallway.

They took Chad to the lab. She handed the signed sheet to the technician. "I need the results immediately. I'll be back in a few minutes."

"Give me at least twenty, okay. I need to get two more out ahead of you."

He wheeled Chad further into the machine-filled room.

Twenty minutes later she looked at the results. He had three broken ribs, a dislocated collar bone, a fractured tibia and brain trauma. He was not conscious.

Chapter 22

Barry looked forward to their early morning breakfasts at the City Diner. He sat in the corner booth, a large law book in front of him. He ordered two coffees. She came in out of the rain shaking her wet hair and hurrying down the aisle shedding her rain coat.

"Coffee." She shivered and wrapped her hands around the warm cup.

He smiled at her. They ordered eggs, bacon and hash browns. The waitress brought a carafe of hot coffee.

"Anything new since last week?" he asked Amy.

She picked at her scrambled eggs. "My mystery patient is still unconscious. It's a month now. I read the police reports. It was an unavoidable accident. It seems two vehicles decided to shift lanes at the same time. John Doe was the second car. He braked to allow the car ahead of him to get into the lane and the trucker behind him couldn't stop fast enough to avoid rear-ending him and sending him down the embankment."

"That's a long time to be unconscious, isn't it? Will he be all right? His other injuries, are they healing?" Barry buttered a piece of wheat toast.

Amy went into a lengthy narration of the prognosis of John Doe. Barry watched her face, the intensity of her eyes, her very turquoise eyes, the little dimple that appeared and disappeared near the corner of her mouth, her even white teeth, and the strands of wispy soft hair that escaped the clasp that held it all back.

"So, relieving that pressure should help him respond. How about you? Any new cases?"

They had become sounding boards to each other. Amy listened but hardly followed the technicalities of the judicial system. Barry would lean toward her, jab the table with his finger to make a legal point, and Amy nodded in agreement, simply enjoying his animated gestures. She admired the confidence he exuded.

"How's your mother, Barry?"

"Doing fine. She walked this week and experienced zero pain." Barry smiled at Amy. "Her Stephen has been to see her twice. She's so happy when he's here with her. I honestly think he is the best medicine for her."

"You know you're right. Sometime people are the best medicine. Like you, Barry. You're good for me. I can tell you anything and you listen. It makes me feel good."

"Let me be truthful, Amy. Half the time I don't know what you're talking about, but it sounds so good." He laughed.

"We're quite a team then. I still don't know a recidivism from a res. But I am so sure that you do."

They finished breakfast and stood outside the diner. The rain was now just a cold mist.

"See you next Sunday, Barry." She turned to go pulling her coat close. He shifted his book under his arm and used his other to stop her.

"Where are you going now?"

"Back to my room to study. I'm free until one this afternoon. I need to shower and study a chapter on the kidneys. You"

He hesitated, looking at her intently. "One of my sort of free days. I have a case study to review…come with me. Let's steal a few hours. I really want to."

She took Barry's hand and they walked three blocks to Barry's off-campus little apartment. He made a fresh pot of coffee, turned up the thermostat and joined Amy on the sofa.

"This is a pretty nice place. I have an efficiency room, but I love it because it's so close to the hospital. You're close, too.

"I leased it from a classmate who's taking a year off to travel in Europe. Speaking of which, did you make it to Ada Venetti's funeral in Bluff View?"

"No, I'm sorry to say I had to miss it. I was just starting my residency and they recognize death of immediate family only. I heard she died while traveling in Sweden. Did you go?"

"I was there for the mass and the burial, then I left. I was there for about seven hours, and flew right back. Muriel Karetsky was there, in a wheelchair. Her daughter Lisa is running the restaurants. She looks a lot like Muriel. Hal Jensen and I went together. He's still at MIT, and Marie Maneros made it. She's working on her second degree in performing arts and musical composition. She wrote a piece of gospel music for the mass. Amy, it was so touching. Marie looks worn out though. Her eyes were so wide, she looked strange. She asked about you and sends her regards."

Amy looked thoughtful. She put her cup on the end table and removed the clasp from her hair, it was damp from the rain. She slipped out of her shoes and tucked her feet under her. Barry laughed out loud.

"Look at us. Two little lambs lost in the woods of academia."

"Not lost, Barry. Just working hard to find our way. A few more obstacles and we will be where we want to be."

He touched her knee, ran his hand down her shin. She knelt on the sofa and leaned into him. She softly kissed his forehead, ruffled his hair and said thickly, "Did this place come with a bed?"

"Yes, queen size. But I only have one pillow.

"Let's see what two super students can do with one pillow," she whispered into his ear.

They made love to the steady beat of the rain hitting the double windows. It was a painful pleasure that exhausted them both. Amy was teasing, insistent, playful and controlled until they both clung to each other in a final gasp of wonder.

"Let's shower."

They soaped each other, explored what they may have missed and reveled in the mixed sensual joy of creamy, liquid shower lotion and cleansing, pulsing streams of warm water.

Over a second cup of coffee they were relaxed and chatty. "I really have to go. See you next Sunday?"

"Amy, about today…."

"No strings, okay?" She stood by the door. He sat at the small table.

"That's what I was hoping you'd say. I have so much to think about at this time in my life."

"Let's freeze the moment. It's there. We can't change it, but we're both moving in different directions. We can enjoy each other without complications. Neither one of us has time to take on excess baggage now. Agree?" She tightened the belt of her raincoat.

"Any other time and well, maybe, eh?" He grinned at her.

"No maybes about it." She winked and left.

Chapter 23

Around the corner from Harvard at Mass General, in a dim, quiet room, Chad Fergis moved his foot. He was aware of moving his foot and that it was his right foot. Trying to move his left foot was impossible and made him tired. After a moment's rest he moved his right foot again wondering why he couldn't move his left foot. He felt like he was squeezing his eyes shut tighter and tighter finally, mercifully, falling back to sleep.

He dreamed of tall pine trees, so tall they blocked out the sun and made the forest floor dim and quiet. There was birdsong all around and the rustling of animals through the soft pine needles, thick and spongy under his feet as he walked purposefully along a winding path. But he had no idea where he was going, even though he knew had to get there because he needed to deliver a message, or was it an order? Some vague idea wandered around his feverish mind, he couldn't grasp it and it made him very sad. He wondered if he would ever find out what he needed to know, what might make his head stop aching and what possibly might help him move his legs that felt like lead as he struggled along the path.

There was a voice, a female voice talking quietly, asking him something. She was speaking softly and gently, an urgency in her tone that he felt was just for him but, try as he might, he couldn't answer. His eyelid was pulled up and a piercing light exploded into his eye then again, in the other eye. The strong desire to moan entered his mind, but even though he constricted his throat muscles, he just couldn't make any kind of sound, not even a soft moan. Someone was rubbing his shoulder, his side, his ankle. He felt a cool hand across his forehead pulling a stray strand of hair back. Just as he moved his right foot, the cover was replaced and he sensed that he was alone again with only feelings of distortion and helplessness. More than anything in the world right now, Chad Fergis wanted that cool hand to stay on his forehead and make everything better. But it was gone.

Chapter 24

Marie Maneros knew that the music department at Penn State was where she had to be. Her musical composition professor, Kyle Rodgers, was, to Marie the superman of her musical studies inspiring her to areas of music she sometimes felt were out of her reach. He was creative, disciplined, understanding, patient and warm all rolled into one.

He was playing Marie's *Ada's Hymn* on an oboe. The class was taking notes. Marie listened carefully as he reached a passage that he had criticized. When he finished, the class agreed, or disagreed, with his appraisal. She heard it played seven different ways, with explanations. She transcribed three into her work sheet. She knew what had to be changed. When the class left, she stayed behind. She picked up a violin, played the passage with the changes, and set the violin back in its case. Kyle Rodgers nodded approvingly at her.

"Perfect. Bravo. Add that one to your portfolio, Marie." He was quietly clapping.

"Thank you, Professor Rodgers. I appreciate the opportunity of having the class react."

"Marie. Take this video. It's an old movie. Watch it without the sound. Then write a score for it. Take a month. You've already aced my class, this will clinch it. Call it an independent study project. You can stop in and see me for consultation as you progress. I think you'll have some fun with a musical challenge such as this."

She took the video, thanked him for his confidence in her work and left. Back in her apartment she began to pace. She felt overly energized to the point of exhaustion. She tidied the small apartment, did some course work and organized her schedule all the while feeling edgy, cold even though the thermostat said seventy one degrees. Both her legs felt odd. She stooped to get a pot from a lower cabinet and couldn't get up from a sitting position on the floor. Nothing hurt but she had no power in her legs. She used a chair to help her finally get up. Sitting at the table, she reached for the ringing phone.

"Marie, this is Amy Crowley. I'm just checking in with you since I haven't heard from you for a while."

"Amy, you're not going to believe this." Marie explained it all to Amy. By the end of her account she was in tears. "I don't know what's happening to me. I feel so helpless."

"I kind of thought you were having a problem. Barry told me he saw you at Ada's funeral and that you didn't look too well. What you've told me confirms my suspicions." Amy's voice was professional now. "Get to a phone book and look for an endocrinologist. It sounds like you may have a common thyroid problem. Hyperactive thyroid, to be specific. They'll do a blood test to see just how much medication to give you to control your iodine level."

"Oh, God, Amy. I have no time to start with doctors," she said.

"Listen, you have to do this right away or it can get serious down the line. A little pill once a day will put you back on track. You'll only have to visit a doctor once every three or four months to check those levels. You'll be fine. And that business with your legs…won't happen again. It's a symptom that occurs only once."

Marie called a doctor in State College and made an appointment for the following Monday afternoon.

"You have the classic symptoms of a hyperactive thyroid. Your blood test shows a high iodine uptake that this prescription will control. One pill a day and make an appointment two months from now for a blood test and a follow-up visit. You'll be fine." The doctor handed her the prescription. Amy had been right on target, smiled Marie.

Feeling much relieved, she returned to campus and went straight to Dr. Rodgers' office. He was leaning over a cello, playing Bach.

"Marie, come in. Having trouble with the video?" He looked at her and she noticed his very blue eyes. How did she miss that striking feature?

"No trouble, Dr. Rodgers. I finished two nights ago." She placed a sheaf of sheet music and the video on his desk.

"Please, call me Kyle. I'm only forty. I was a child prodigy." He leaned back and laughed. "Sit. You seem distracted."

She told him of her recent medical episode. "I don't know how accurate my music will be now," she spoke softly. "Maybe this will affect my work."

He set the cello on a stand and stood up. He paced around the office. "Your music comes from inside of you, no matter what else is there. You're a channel for the music you create for others to enjoy. I recognize that in you, Marie. You must be aware of it, too. Historically, there have been musicians who have been blind, deaf, even mad, but their music had to be released. You know that, though. I have seen your grades in all your courses including Music in History."

He smiled at her. "Do you need lunch? You look tired."

"I don't feel tired. I feel relaxed, for the first time in months. And you have made me feel better by putting my little problem in perspective. I must have sounded like a baby." She rose and said, "Yes, let's have lunch."

He locked the office behind them.

Chapter 25

Chad Fergis opened his eyes nine weeks after he lost consciousness. First, he was aware of a blue light dancing across his closed lids. He slowly opened his eyes to a thin squint. The blue light became stronger. He opened wider. He realized that the light was from a television set in the corner of the room. He slowly began to gaze around his bed. He knew he was in a hospital. There was a nightstand with a water pitcher next to his bed. The matching tumbler had a bent straw in it. There was a wide window on one side of the room, a cream-colored curtain stretched across the length of his bed. Outside the window he could see part of a red brick building and some clouds. His side hurt. His head felt compressed. He knew he could move his right leg. His left one felt like it wasn't there.

Her pager went off when she was with Barry. She glanced at it quickly. "It's the hospital. I have to go." She pecked him on the cheek, dressed quickly, and literally ran out the door.

"See you, doc," he mumbled into the pillow, then headed for the shower.

Chapter 26

Amy opened the door to John Doe's room and briskly went to the side of Dr. Cage.

"How long has he been awake?" she asked.

"I came in on rounds about an hour ago. His eyes were open. Vitals are pretty good, but he's unresponsive." Dr. Cage spoke softly. "We'll continue the same meds. In the meantime, I've arranged for more tests. Do you have time to take him to the lab?"

"Very little, but I'll stay as long as I can. I start on the ortho ward tonight."

She pulled up a stool and sat next to the bed. Dr. Cage left. Amy looked at Chad Fergis and smiled. He looked back at her. His eyes were bruised and bloodshot, but somehow those eyes were trying to communicate. Amy saw questions in his eyes, a sadness, a wondering. A wave of compassion flooded her. If only she could interpret the intelligence of those eyes.

"Can you speak?" she asked. She took his hand and felt his pulse. It didn't change. No response from Chad.

He thought he recognized her voice. What was she saying? Why couldn't he focus or speak? She pulled a tissue out of the box and wiped his lips and dabbed around his eyes.

"You're coming back, buddy. You're going to be just fine. I'll be back as soon as I can." Amy ran her fingers through his dark wavy hair.

It was soft. She was glad the nurse's aid was keeping him clean as she ordered. She rose to leave and thought she saw panic in his eyes. They widened and looked pained.

"I'll be back. Real soon. I'll be taking you to the lab."

She stopped at the nurse's station and wrote on John Doe's record noting that his eyes were bloodshot, that he was awake but unresponsive. No speech.

"Is the John Doe coming to life, Dr. Crowley? I heard he was awake."

"No, Bonnie. Nothing. Totally silent. He's a real strong, silent type. Weird, isn't it?" She handed the record back to Bonnie.

"Nothing in his personal effects?"

"What personal affects?"

"The policeman brought a tan envelope. Said it was what they had found around the wreckage. And what about the lady that called? Martha something. Did you ever call her?"

Amy stared at Susan. "Let's go slow, nurse. Tell me all about this, from the top."

"Well, after John Doe was admitted, a police officer brought the envelope. He told me what it was. I put your name on it and had a candy striper take it to the ER. I knew you were still on assignment there, so I thought you'd get it the next time you came on shift." She blushed a deep shade of pink.

"And the lady that called? Tell me about that."

"She didn't call here. I assume she was calling police along the route her cousin, that's who she was looking for, would take. He was days late getting to her house and she was worried. Since our John Doe fit the description she gave the police, an officer told her that he would contact someone from the hospital to give her a call to verify her description. She must have thought it was a mistake since no one called her." Her voice dropped.

"So the note, the phone message from the police officer was sent to ER too?" Amy didn't wait for an answer. She rushed to the ER nurses' station.

"Where are patients' belongings?" she asked a doctor who was filling a chart.

"I don't know," he shrugged.

She went through the papers in the wire baskets scattered around the desk. She went to a locker behind a lab door. She frantically moved objects around looking for a tan envelope, and she found it, under a torn, battered backpack. She went to the desk again, and began searching drawers.

The young doctor watched her for a moment then asked, "What was it you were looking for?"

"An envelope with my name on it. Dr. Amy Crowley. We have a John Doe who was comatose for nine weeks. It may be a clue to his identity," Amy continued to open and shut drawers.

He went to an alcove around one corner of the ER. There was a small desk and file cabinet there. On top of the cabinet was a wire basket half full of envelopes, single pages, paper-clipped memos and notes.

"I once found a memo to me in that basket. A week after a meeting I was supposed to attend. This is a frantic place and sometimes mail just doesn't seem important." He pushed papers around. It wasn't there.

Chapter 27

The room dimmed as evening came. The brightness that came through the window faded as daylight turned to night. The TV was off, so the flickering light from the set was gone. Soft yellow light filtered in from the hallway. Chad squeezed his eyes shut then slowly opened them. He was alone. He tried to make a sound in his throat, like a moan, or a cough. He succeeded in producing a deep raspy growl. He closed his eyes and dreamed of mountains and pine trees.

Chapter 28

"Barry, help me with this stuff." She had the contents from the police envelope spread across the table. It was all burned black, hard mud encrusted and anything soft was shredded. He left his law book on the sofa and padded over to the table in his bare feet. His black hair was disheveled, his robe open revealing black curly chest hair. He picked up a piece of cloth and smoothed it on the table. He looked across at her.

"This looks like a black and red hunting shirt. Well it was, once. The kind you get from L.L. Bean. It has a padded lining. I used to have a black and white one. Was he wearing this?"

"The police report said it was stuck to his bare skin. He was He was pulled and tugged out of the car after it flipped and rolled. I guess there was a lot of back and forth and sideways violence before the car finally stopped upside down."

They tried to open a burned and fused wallet. Any plastic had melted so not only was it burnt brittle, it was a solid block of hardened plastic. Barry used a flat knife to try to pry open the edges. He succeeded in shredding cards into powder.

"Wait. Pull this edge a little more." She looked hard at an 'I' and an 's' and a '46'. The rest was illegible.

"I should have taken this to the lab. Maybe there's something they could do, but I doubt it. They found this watch in the grass, too. I guess it was his since it's so battered and charred."

Barry picked up the watch by the broken metal elasticized band. The face piece was shattered, the clock face scored and blackened. On the charred and dented back she could make out, "To Bos, Go" and the rest was unreadable.

She blew out an air of frustration. Barry came around to the back of her chair, kissed her neck and said, "Maybe he'll just tell you when he snaps out of it. I have to go now."

Amy reached up and held his arm. "I saw your mom yesterday. She's doing fine. I was on rounds with the orthopedic team. They are pleased with her progress. She has a great upbeat attitude. I met her young man, too. You were right. He dotes on her, makes her happy."

Barry smiled. "He does. I'm kind of getting used to the idea." He ruffled her hair. "You?"

"I suppose so. Ceil and my dad have been to Florida twice, on a cruise to the western Caribbean, even to Sea World. He's having fun again. They'll probably relocate to Florida some day. I'm okay with it for now."

Barry laughed and headed for the shower. She gathered up the debris called personal effects and placed them back in the tan envelope. There was a pen which advertised Northern Evergreen Industries, a broken pair of Ray Bans, the watch and some loose change. She stared at the back again. Boswell? Boston? A nickname like Bosco? Maybe he'd wake up and tell her.

Chapter 29

At her apartment she repeated her study of bone structure and diseases of the bones. She had to be ready for the rapid-fire questions aimed at the interns during rounds. It got late. She had two hours before returning to the wards. Her phone rang.

"Marie? Is everything all right?"

Marie sounded far away. "Amy, I owe you so much. You were right. It was my thyroid and since I'm taking the little white pill which I can't pronounce, it's under control and I'm doing fine. Thank you, thank you." She sounded so happy.

"It's almost midnight. I'm getting ready to go on night duty. Isn't this kind

of late for you? Where are you? You sound far away." Amy sounded concerned.

"Oh gosh, Amy. It's seven a.m. here. I'm sorry. We just finished breakfast. I forgot about the time difference."

"Where are you and who's 'we'?"

"I'm in Belgium on a music institute grant. I'm here to study classics. It's a six-week series of seminars by composers, conductors and artists from all over Europe. My composition and arrangement professor, Dr. Kyle Rodgers got the grant and invited me to accompany him. Since I'm getting credits for it, I agreed to go," she said.

"So you're not with a group? You're traveling with this teacher? Just the two of you?"

"I'm okay with it, Amy. He's great. Kyle is forty. He was a child prodigy. He knows so much about music. I have a lot of respect for him." She was blushing over the phone.

"The important thing, young lady, is does he have respect for you?"

"Yes, Mommy. He really does. I have never met a more considerate person. Not that I'm using him for mucho credits, but he has so many contacts in this field, useful contacts that he's making mine, too. He's invaluable," she said confidently.

And you're no longer a virgin, Amy thought to herself. "Well, enjoy the rest of your trip but please be careful. Don't forget to take that pill every day, along with the other pill you should be taking, too. Call me when you get back."

"I will, I promise. And please don't worry."

Chapter 30

The barn was painted brick red with all doors and trim painted white. It was a rambling horse barn, well-tended and manicured. Above the main aisle of stalls, in white letters was –W. The –W or Bar W was the Wilson's brand. They had been raising thoroughbred horses for over thirty years.

Inside, Martha Wilson brushed the chestnut horse. The coat was shiny and healthy. Its long champagne mane and tail were smooth and silky. She loved *Star*. It was her favorite. She hung up the brush and walked between the stalls. One of the handlers was raking up straw.

"Morning, Martha. Hear anything?" Eric leaned on his rake.

"No, Eric. I called every trooper station along his route. No luck." She tapped her foot against the stall door.

"Maybe he just decided to take a last minute side trip somewhere. He's been in the woods for so long maybe he's overwhelmed by all the activity around him. He'll show up, you'll see."

"Thanks, Eric. I'll let you know if I hear anything." She walked out to the racing oval. Two of their fillies were being timed as they thundered down the track. Martha remembered how Chad loved to be around the thoroughbreds.

"How they doing, Phil?" She hiked a leg up on the lower fence rail and leaned against the trainer. He held the stop watch to her and raised his eyebrows.

"Best time so far on *Blaze*. She's going to make you a lot of money.

Take my word for it, Martha. That's a horse with a lot of heart." He looked at her. "Nothing yet, eh?"

She put her head down. "No. And I don't know what else I can do. Just wait, I guess, and hope he shows up someplace."

"Don't you lose hope. Just remember that he's a very capable young man. I'm sure there is a very good reason why he's late."

She turned and headed back to the ranch house.

"Martha, come and eat something." Sue Wilson had pancakes and syrup on the table. She began to pour coffee. "Sit down. Have a bite to eat."

"I can't stop thinking about Chad. It's been too long. Something bad is going on. I know it."

"You did everything you could. Now it's up to him. You made all those calls and got nothing. I'd say he got side-tracked. Maybe he met a woman. Our Chad is one handsome young man, you know." Sue put butter on the table. She eased back into the chair, leaned over and patted Martha's hand. "I love the way you care for everyone in this family. Mark just shrugged when he heard that Chad was late. It's his cousin, for God's sake."

"Sue, he's my cousin, too. I married all of you, you know. Mark wasn't in the tack barn or at the track. Where is he?" Martha asked about her husband.

"He drove into town to get orange juice. That's my boy. Just like his dad was. Couldn't start the day without his juice. Like it was magic or something," chuckled Sue. She had a wide smile and eyes that shone. Her curly blond and grey hair was pulled back in a soft bun. She spilled syrup on her pancakes and smiled at her daughter-in-law.

"I hear you. He is set in his ways for a thirty-year old, isn't he? You know, I think you may be right. The only lead I got was from that trooper who said that an accident victim they took to Mass. General Hospital fit Chad's description. Since I never heard from them, I guess it wasn't Chad. Someone from there could have at least called me back, though, don't you think? Mark says they're busy in emergency rooms and probably just didn't think it was important to call back and say that it wasn't Chad. You're probably both right." She put her head on her fist and picked at her cranberry walnut pancakes.

Chapter 31

It was raining hard outside. Huge drops pelted the window and melted down the grey glass in rapid rivulets. Amy sat next to the bed. She took his hand, looked into his eyes and said, "I think you can understand me. Dr. Cage said you can move your leg. Can you move your hand?" There was a hesitation, then a faint squeeze of her hand.

"Good. Now, I'm going to ask you some questions. One squeeze for yes, two for no. Do you understand?" She felt a faint response, a slow tightening of her hand.

She placed the envelope on the bed and pulled out the pen. "Did you ever hear of Northern Evergreen Industries?" Two short pulses.

Next, she reached for the watch. She held it up for him to see. "Is this your watch?" His eyes opened wide as he stared at the distorted, charred watch. "Is it yours? Do you recognize it?" He slowly squeezed her hand two times. She decided not to show him the piece of Woolrich cloth.

"Is your name Bo, or something like Boswell, Boscov, or Bosley?" He hesitated, then firmly pressed twice.

"Do you know your name?" He squinted at her hard, his brow wrinkled as he relaxed his hand. He slowly moved his head back and forth signifying a negative answer.

Amy patted his shoulder. "I'll be back. I'm a resident doctor here so I don't have much time, but I'll be back. I'm Dr. Amy Crowley. I was working the ER the afternoon they brought you in. You'll start to remember, I promise you. It will all come back. This is only temporary." She ran her cool hand across his forehead.

She stared at him as his bruised head slowly nodded a yes.

"Good. Any movement you can make is a good sign. Keep trying, Bosley. Keep trying."

He opened his eyes wide and moved his head left and right and frowned at her.

"Not Bosley, eh? Okay. I'll come up with a better one. You do look like a Bosley, though." She adjusted his pillow and turned on the TV to a Patriot's game.

After she left the room, he turned his head to the window and watched the rain beading and streaming down the window. He stared at the television for a while and a thought entered his mind. Someone was speaking. "How 'bout them Eagles? What a team. They're goin' all the way." The fellow was skinny, but tanned and hearty. He chewed tobacco and spit on the leaves. His name was almost there, Chad tried to grasp it. The guy wore a yellow hard hat and an orange jacket. Chad could make out the letters G.F. on the pocket.

Trying valiantly to hold onto the image, his eyes grew tired.. He leaned back against the cool pillow and fell asleep.

Chapter 32

Amy returned to her apartment after a double shift. She was exhausted. After a shower and a microwave dinner, she settled on the sofa to study for tomorrow's rounds. It would be the cardiac wing, so study was a must.

After a chapter on stents, she started to prepare a cup of tea. One more chapter, then I better get some sleep. The little doorbell chimed. Amy peered through the peephole. It was Barry. She opened the door and he tumbled into her.

"Are you drunk?"

"Nah. I just had a bottle of wine I was saving for us but you weren't home. I called and called…" His speech was slurred.

"A whole bottle of wine? Did you drive here?"

"No, no. Wouldn't think of it my little chickadee. Let's go to bed." He reached for her.

Amy started coffee. He started to undress.

"What brought on the celebration, Barry?" She was stern but not angry.

"Oh. I got some good news. Got a job offer in the New York City prosecutor's office. How about that?" He threw his pants on the sofa and began unbuttoning his shirt. He swayed ever so slightly.

"But what about finishing here? Won't that put you behind your schedule?" She poured two cups. She didn't even put out the cream and sugar.

"Got it all under control, sweetie." He grinned widely at her. "I go on independent study. Ha. It's what I'm already doing. But I'll be getting paid and be earning credits, too. I come back here for graduation and I take my bar exam on schedule. Then I'll be Barry Kretzler, Esquire." He threw his arms out wide and spun around the room until he flopped on the sofa.

Amy giggled. He sounded like Groucho Marx. "How did you pull this off, Barry?"

"Remember, honey bunny," he put his hand to his chest, "I worked there and I made a lot of contacts, serious contacts. I have a detective who has been my friend since I was a youngster, a kid," his voice dropped. Both hands went to his face and he began sobbing.

"Barry?" She rose and went to him. His body shook, his sobs were deep and full of pain. She wrapped her arms around him and rubbed his back.

He buried his head in her shoulder and cried into her hair. "I just wish my father could be here for this giant step. I wish…" He sobbed again.

She hugged him tighter. "We're both worn out and you've taken too much of your edge off." Amy took his hand and led him to her bed. He was snoring in moments. She set the alarm for five a.m. and crawled under the covers with him. She traced his shoulders, his chest, his abdomen, loving the hardness of his body. Well, most of it anyway.

She whispered in his ear, "Alcohol is not an aphrodisiac, Barry." She smiled, turned over and slept soundly.

Chapter 33

Fran Kretzler sat up in a recliner in the corner of her hospital room as Barry told her his news. She was elated.

"You'll be in Manhattan. That's wonderful news. When does your job start?" Fran reached to Barry. He took her hand.

"Monday, Mom. Amy here tells me you're going to be released on Thursday. We'll go home together. I have some loose ends to tie up at school anyway. But I want you to know that I'll be looking for an apartment, maybe in Westchester or White Plains. I'll stay with you until you're ready to go back to work."

"Oh, Barry, I'm so glad you want to be independent. You can start looking for a place right away. I'll be fine." She primped her hair.

From the doorway, Michael Harland said quietly, "I hope it's okay, but I'll be taking care of Frances. It will be my pleasure."

Barry turned, walked over to Michael and shook his hand. "I see, Mike. Are you two going to give me a chance to find a place at all? Or are my things already in the front yard?"

Michael paled. "It's your home. I just meant you didn't have to worry about your mom. I live with my daughter and her family. I can move out whenever I want. Time is not an issue here. Your mom and I just want to be together now. We don't mean to be pushy."

"I know. It's great. I really am glad for you both." He looked at Michael. "I assume you'll be taking Mom home, then?"

They both nodded their assent.

Amy had been at the door quietly watching the scene unfold. She looked at her watch and said, "I need to continue rounds. Barry, I'll see you later. Good luck to you, Mrs. Kretzler." She nodded at Michael and left. As she walked down the hallway, a tear found its way down her cheek. She walked briskly, wiping the moisture away with her sleeve. She thought of her dad and Ceil, the turmoil they knew they were causing her, and their helplessness to change it. She vowed to make their giant step a little easier to take. She'd start with wiring them a dozen roses.

Barry sat on the edge of the bed. "I'll be home on Saturday then. I'll start work on Monday and begin looking at the house ads."

"If you like, my niece is with a private real estate firm in Tarrytown. They are on the multiple listing service so all the available rentals are on her computer. If you tell her what you're looking for, your price range and location, she can give you a print out of prospective properties."

Barry laughed, "I'm getting a picture here, you two. And I'm not in it."

"Don't be so silly," Fran said. She laughed through her words. Michael put his hand on her shoulder and she covered it with her own. Barry could see they were smitten with each other and he'd be a third wheel. He suddenly missed Amy.

Chapter 34

The nurses' station was quiet for the last few minutes. Susan used the time to catch up on folder work. It was a never-ending chore so the free minutes were precious. The technician was tapping the counter in front of her with an envelope.

"Yes?" Susan was curt because she was harried.

"You know this doc? I found this letter under an X-Ray pad I was moving out. We got a new machine. It's about time, too. That old one was on its last legs. Never really dependable," he went on. He pushed the envelope across the counter.

Susan took the letter and saw it was addressed to Dr. Crowley. She picked up the phone and pressed the intercom button. "Dr. Crowley, please report to the seventh floor nurses' station."

She waited, hoping that Dr. Crowley was on duty and in range of the intercom. In the meantime, she called the central operator and asked for a number for Dr. Amy Crowley. After fifteen minutes, and a second page, she dialed Amy's number. It was a few minutes after noon.

"Hello," Amy answered the phone briskly.

"Dr. Crowley, it's Susan. Seventh floor nurses' station." She took a deep breath. "I have your missing envelope. The one on the John Doe. An X-Ray technician found it under a…."

"I'll be right there." Amy hung up.

Susan stared at the phone. "You're welcome," she said into the dead line.

Chapter 35

Amy stood at the counter with the police report spread out in front of her. The description fit. Mrs. Martha Wilson of Kensworth, W. Va. was searching for her cousin, Chad Fergis of Elk Pond, Maine. He was to visit her on or about May 4. He was a week late. Now, Amy thought, he's about three months late. She reached for the phone and called the number on the police report.

"Mrs. Wilson, please. Mrs. Martha Wilson." Amy sounded professional.

"This is Martha Wilson. What can I do for you?"

"This is Amy Crowley from Massachusetts General Hospital in Cambridge. I have a police report…"

"My God. That was three months ago. Is my cousin there then? Why did you wait so long to call back?" Martha was annoyed, excited and angry, but elated, all at once. She called out, "Mom, Mark, it's about Chad."

"I apologize for the delay. The letter was routed through the hospital and ended up hidden in the X-ray lab. Believe me, your anger is appreciated. I've already chewed some heads off, but in our defense, Mrs. Wilson, this is a very busy place where patients are the first priority. The police report and your number would have been a tremendous help to us. I know it's late, but please, I am so sorry for all your trouble. You should know that your cousin has been receiving the best of care."

"How is he, Dr. Crowley?"

"Let's be sure we have the right man first. Can you tell me anything about his body that would be a positive i.d.? Scars? Birthmarks?"

Martha hesitated a moment. She was talking to someone near the phone.

"He should have a scar behind his right ear, two on his upper right shoulder about three inches long, a dent in his left shin bone and uneven knuckles on his right hand. All these are logging injuries from falling limbs, logging equipment, that kind of thing. Those are the ones we remember, there could be more."

Amy was taking notes. "Anything else?"

"Are his eyes open?" asked Martha.

"He was in a coma until about a week ago. He can't speak, but he responds to questions by squeezing hands. His eyes do open occasionally, but most of the time he sleeps."

Martha skipped a second, then said, "Next time he opens his eyes notice the gold flecks around the irises. I don't want to sound like I'm bragging, but his eyes are incredible and his lashes are like a mile long. I know, I'm biased, but our cousin is one handsome man."

"It sounds like your cousin is here, Mrs. Wilson. He has a long way to go, but he's healing well. However, he seems to be suffering from amnesia, common after a head trauma. Maybe if you could visit him, it might jog his memory."

"I feel like jumping in the car right now, but we run a ranch here in West Virginia, my husband, mother-in-law and I. A horse ranch of thoroughbreds, you see. People have a lot of money tied up in our studs. Two of the horses are ready to foal. It's a busy time, but by the beginning of next week I will be there at his side. You tell Chad that Martha and Aunt Sue will be there soon, okay?"

"I'll do that. So his name is Chad. Why would he have a watch with 'to Bos' on it?"

"Oh. The men that work for him at his logging company gave it to him when he sold the business. He told me it was engraved *To Boss. Good Luck from all of us.* It was his going away gift. He was going to Washington to take a position with the National Park Service, something he always wanted to do after he finished forestry school. Then, of course...." She choked.

"Mrs. Wilson, I'm going to use all the information you gave me. It's a good start toward helping him remember his past. I'm sure that family will be his best medicine though. I look forward to meeting you next week. He's in room 704 by the way." Amy hung up. She began scanning the notes she just took.

Chapter 36

Chad knew if he tried he could speak. It was almost as if he was afraid to disturb his throat. Dr. Cage had just said his throat was healed and speaking should follow soon. He sipped the cool water the nurse offered him. It felt soothing as it flowed down. Dr. Cage was changing a bandage on his chest.

"Ribs are healing nicely, too," he muttered. "You're doing fine, young man but you're not out of the woods just yet."

The words puzzled Chad. Like he should recognize them. *Not out of the woods yet.* The words stayed in his mind. He frowned, he couldn't reach the meaning. But it was something he should know, he mused. It had something to do with being in the forest with tall pine trees and maybe chain saws, or big machines to cut down trees.

"No scar tissue on your head wounds." He moved his fingers around the back of Chad's head.

Chad's voice cracked and wheezed. It was a Herculean effort and it sounded terrible. "How long have I been here?"

"Good going. The more you speak the easier it will get. It's been about three months now. You were in a coma most of that time. You have a name for us?"

"No, sir. The lady doc calls me Bosley," he croaked. "Could that be my name?"

"Oh. Dr. Crowley. She said your watch has Bos on the back. Anything to do with Boston?"

"I don't know." His voice was deep and hollow that time, less of a rasp, more of a deep, hollow cavernous tone. Chad hated the way he sounded, but he knew it was important to speak, as the doctor said.

Dr. Cage patted his arm, "Don't worry about it. You'll get it back soon. Every day will bring you more and more images, things to remember and eventually to make you all better. Healing in the brain takes a while. There doesn't seem to be any permanent damage, though. So you should start to recall quite a lot in a few days. Just don't rush it. Let it all happen at its own speed. You're a healthy, though banged up, young man. You'll do just fine. Dr. Crowley has been right on top of your case ever since you came into emergency. Don't hesitate to lean on her. She's a fine doctor."

Chad leaned back and closed his eyes. He was extremely tired.

Chapter 37

Barry combed his black wavy hair back, buttoned his white shirt and arranged his silver and blue striped tie. Fran stood in the doorway and watched him for a moment.

"You look nice, Barry. You excited?" She stepped forward and folded down his collar in back.

"You know, since working at the court house for the past few years, this feels right somehow. Like it's where I belong. I'm sure they'll give me some grunt work at first, but I have a plan, Mom. Some day I'll move from a cubicle to an office. But, hey, look at you. No walker?" He hugged his mom. "Where are you off to all dolled up?"

Her cheeks turned pink. "Michael is picking me up for lunch. We have some talking to take care of." She pushed her hair back. She looked great to Barry. He smiled at her as he slipped into his sport coat.

"So, don't leave me in the dark. When's the big day? The day after I move out?" He chuckled.

"I don't know. We both feel a little guilty, you know. It's such a big step for both of us. I get a little scared of all the changes that have happened to me over the last few years." Her voice grew soft, almost a whisper. "And lately we've been talking about relocating."

Barry stopped combing his hair. "Wow, Mom, all these sudden bombshells. I don't know if I can take it. You don't like Yonkers anymore? Where? New Jersey?"

"Arizona, Barry. We've been looking into it for a while now. Sun City, Arizona. My cousin, Betty is there and Michael has two brothers there. It sounds ideal. I have computer skills and medical organization background. It should be easy for me to find a little job to keep me busy. Michael's friend is chief of maintenance at one of the golf courses and he told Mike he could always use some help. Michael is very good with machinery and landscaping, he loves plants. He'd fit right in at the golf course. So we'd be occupied, make some new friends and travel a little."

He hugged her. "Sounds like you've worked it all out. Just be happy and lose the guilt feelings, okay? It's been ten, eleven years now. You were a good wife to Dad. Now you deserve some happiness."

"You're a good son. I know you'll do good things in your career. Now, I have to get ready."

He buttoned his jacket. "I'll be late. Mike's niece is showing me a place in White Plains and two in Westchester. I'm sure he told her to use her best real estate skills to sell me one of those places already." He winked at Fran as he went out the door.

That afternoon around three, Barry was busy going through case files, organizing folders by dates, when there was a tap at the side of his cubicle. A familiar figure pushed into the small space and squeezed into the chair across from Barry. It was Detective Matt Harrison. Recognition came quickly. Barry remembered him having the widest shoulders he had ever seen. His hair was still buzz cut, though splashed with grey, his face wide. He smiled at Barry holding some folders close to his chest.

"Detective Harrison. Long time." Barry put down his pencil and closed the folder he had been shuffling through.

"See you got a job right in the middle of all the action. Congratulations. You done with school?"

"Not quite. This counts." He waved his hand around the cubicle. "Life experience. And I'm on independent study until the bar exam so my nose is still stuck in the books."

"I'm getting ready to retire," Harrison said. He plopped three folders on the little desk. "My collection of sleaze. I copied the files on

Machlich and Appleby. They've been busy little boys. They served some time, a year, then later, eighteen months. They're like two eels, though. There's always a question of guilt, a witness who turns, stuff like that. Keep the files. The new stuff will come through here. Copy it and keep the file up to date. They need to be off the streets permanently. It's just a matter of time. They'll slip up because they're getting meaner with age. You're in a position now to keep tabs on them and word around the court house is that one day soon, you'll have your credentials to step into a slot that can do those boys some real harm if they ever come before you, know what I mean? So you work hard, get to the top of the heap and get rid of the bottom feeders that the police will drag in front of you.

"I really appreciate this, Detective Harrison. I promise to do all I can to achieve just that. I'm not that nervous little kid that threatened them years ago. I'm working on getting some real clout. My ultimate goal is a judgeship or even N.Y. D.A. Barry stood and shook the detective's hand. "Good luck to you, sir."

"Here's my card. If you need anything, or if you get anything, call me, okay? And I will watch your progress. The grapevine around here is pretty accurate." He placed his card on the desk and left. Barry picked up the first folder, leaned back and began to get all caught up.

Chapter 38

Behind closed eyelids, Chad was aware of a presence, an antiseptic odor mixed with a citrus shampoo. He slowly opened his eyes. Amy was on the stool next to the bed. Her hair was pulled back with a clasp, a stethoscope hung around her neck.

"We're moving into August, Bosley. I need you to snap out of it, okay?" She was smiling at him, but something in her tone made him know she was serious.

"Not Bosley," his new voice croaked. He struggled and again forced out, "Not Bosley."

"I know. I'm teasing. Sounds good to hear your voice, though. I'm sure you sound more like Garth Brooks, or maybe Elvis. This voice is temporary. Can I read off some names to you? See if anything triggers a recall?" She held up a notepad.

"Sure. Go ahead." He shifted slightly against the pillow.

"Did anyone ever tell you that you have incredible eyes, hazel flecked with gold, super long lashes?"

"I don't think so. Do I?"

"Well not right now. They're sort of a greenish bruise. Kind of scratched up too. But Martha Wilson told me all about your eyes. Do you know Martha Wilson? She's your cousin from Kensworth, West Virginia. Has a thoroughbred race horse farm, the –W. You were going to stop there on your way to D.C. Sound familiar?" Amy looked up from her notes.

He squinted at her. His brow furrowed. "No, none of it."

She's coming to visit you the early part of next week. Also your Aunt Sue. Martha said you call her Tia Sue. You took a Spanish class once and that's all you took away from it. Tia Sue and Tio Fredericko, your Uncle Fred when he was alive."

He shook his head no. He looked so defeated Amy was tempted to fold the notebook and try again another time but she decided she had to push on in case one of the items jogged a memory.

"How about this...you own Gene Fergis Logging in Elk Pond, Maine. You just sold the family business to Evergreen Northern Industries. You were driving to Washington to take a job with the National Park Service. What are you going to be, like Smokey the Bear with a big hat or something?"

"You're pretty funny, doc. I don't know your story, though..."

"I'm just trying to set something free here. You have a lot of little scars that Martha says are logging accidents. Do you remember any trees falling on you?"

He rolled his head to the side. "I'm tired."

She reached into her pocket and pulled out the watch. "You're Chad Fergis. The Bos on the watch is for Boss. The inscription was 'To Boss, Good Luck from all of us.' Bet they all chipped in about a dollar." She held the broken, charred watch between them.

He smiled. "It's a Stauer. I guess I paid the men pretty well." He stared at the watch for a moment then returned to turning his head away.

Amy put the watch back in her pocket. "Dr. Cage and I are recommending a physical therapist and a psychologist to work with you starting tomorrow. It will help you recover much faster than my feeble attempts." She smoothed the covers across his chest.

"Can I afford it?" he asked.

"You can pay all your bills here with ease, Mr. Chad Fergis. Northern Evergreen agreed to seven hundred thousand a year for five years. Hey, I'm going to bill you too, buddy." She laughed and left him smiling.

He leaned back. Trees. They're so familiar, those big, green trees.

He closed his eyes and could see the skinny man in his mind. The hard hat tugged at him, as did the orange jacket. In the distance he could hear heavy machinery. The man was hoisting himself onto a large green tractor, engine rumbling and gears grinding. He spit a stream of brown tobacco juice down into the pine debris. Chad reached for the memory, the man was laughing, it was slipping away. The man shouted something over the drone of the machinery. It faded.

Chapter 39

They settled into their first class seats and waited patiently for the engines to rev and the plane to take off. Marie kicked off her shoes and stretched her arms out in front of her. She was grinning like a schoolgirl.

"We are returning in triumph, dear girl. Let's create a symphony when we get back to the university. We'll dedicate it to the great maestros of Europe." Kyle was animated, full of electric energy.

"How can I ever thank you. All we did, and credits, too. I have a briefcase full of wonder. We were so lucky to get into the archives of so many *Academia Musicas.* I'm so excited about the lost passages of Chopin, hymns by Bach, ideas, ideas. We should do this every year. What places." Marie leaned into him. She put her head on his shoulder, put her arm through his and squeezed.

Kyle looked down at her. "Are you all right, Marie? You look a little tired. We can get the next flight, you know." He took her hand. "You could rest for a few hours. You could lie down."

"I'm fine," she sighed. "Honest, I really can't wait to get back."

"I noticed that you didn't stop studying at all on this trip. Think you're ready for the performing arts test?"

"Yes, I am," she said confidently. "I have some show tunes ready and the score from one of the scenes from *Ring of Fire.* As soon as I tape it all, I'll let you be the judge." She kissed his fingers.

"As usual, it will be brilliant. Thanks to my direction, of course," he said. His eyes crinkled.

Marie noticed the fine lines around his eyes. She wondered if he was the one who was tired and needed to rest for a few hours. Maybe I'm being selfish she thought. Their plane was scheduled to take off from Heathrow at noon, but there was another at six. The hotel was just a short distance from the airport. They just had breakfast. If they skipped lunch, they could relax and head out at four.

"Kyle, on second thought, maybe we could take the six o'clock flight. The program last night was long and at times the London Symphony was a bit heavy." They left the plane and headed to the counter where they arranged to have their luggage go without them. They would be taking the next flight.

The hotel was lovely. She stood on the balcony and looked out over the Thames and Parliament. So much history, she thought. Kyle made them drinks, she slipped off her shoes. Next to him on the bed, he unbuttoned her blouse and pulled down her bra straps. She took his drink and put both on the side table, let her skirt drop and lay back on the plump pillows. He watched her, then lay back next to her.

Under the covers, the musician's fingers produced a concerto of soft moans and purrs of pleasure. Kyle caressed her gently, kissed her passionately, and she guided him into her with sweet tedeums of ecstatic groans. Their opus reached a crescendo of pulsating percussions. Spent, they finally rested as planned.

On the plane, Marie was flushed with excitement. They shared a light snack.

Kyle reached into his jacket pocket. "Take this card. If you ever want to create scores for a living, call this fellow. He's a friend of mine, a former student, actually, who works as a manager for a new production company. It's based in Beverly Hills, but they have a branch in New York. I've been feeding him some of your work and he's very impressed. I know he's interested. Get your degrees, of course, Arranging, Performing Arts, Composing. Get the masters in Performing Arts. That's where your strength lies. It'll be another six months or so, but it will be invaluable." He sighed and leaned back, crossing his arms loosely in his lap.

Marie took the card. Paul Andrews was a production manager at Blue Dreams Studio. She put the card in her new Italian leather purse. Kyle was so generous but right now he looked so tired and drawn. She felt a little guilty for having him take her to just about every musical event in Europe, but the lessons she learned would last her a lifetime and she promised to take this trip again in the future when all the studying was over and they could simply enjoy Europe and each other.

Chapter 40

He heard the whispering outside his door. Chad was aware of female voices that he was sure he did not recognize. He rolled his head to the side and feigned sleep.

"It's me, Chad, Tia Sue and Martha. How do you feel?" She spoke quietly. They stood by the bed, uncertain. Chad was sure these people were sincerely trying to help him. He turned his head to them and smiled, enjoying the comfort of their nearness. Sue looked homey and pleasant, Martha seemed cute, bouncy and sisterly.

"Thanks for coming. Dr. Crowley told me about you both, but," he coughed softly, "I really don't know you. Did we spend a lot of time together? Should I know you well?"

Martha came closer. She took his hand. "You spent summers on our ranch until you were old enough to work with your dad and Grampa Gene. We kept in touch, though, calling each other with all kinds of news. I wish you could remember us. We're the only family you have since your dad passed away.

He shook his head. "Wish I could place you. You're both very nice. It's comforting to know that I have someone who cares. I appreciate this visit. Dr. Crowley said that one of your horses foaled. Everything okay?"

Sue smiled at him. "Great. It was a colt that Martha here named *Chaos*. He looks like a real winner, a feisty animal."

"Do you remember a horse named *Lightning*, a mare? It was one of our fastest horses. You used to love galloping around the oval in the mornings, early, before we were awake. It was dark brown with a gold mane and tail and it had a jagged streak between its eyes. You loved that horse, even when it threw you." Martha laughed as she eagerly told him the story of the mare. Chad stared at Martha. His fingers clenched the sheets, he frowned and his eyes went wide.

"Are you all right?" Sue Wilson touched her nephew's shoulder. He shivered.

His voice became low and husky, struggling with the words. "I can see that horse. It has a red saddle and the reins are black. The mane was soft and shiny."

"That's right, honey." Sue looked at Martha. They both raised their eyebrows and smiled knowing they were witnessing a breakthrough.

"Do you remember riding her?" asked Martha. "She was easy to handle."

"Yeah, I think I do. I need time, but I did get that picture. I can see *Lightning* all right. A pretty horse. The oval was a mile and we'd go around three times before the horse slowed. I can see the barn, too, with the stalls." His voice was tired.

Martha gave him some water. He leaned back against the pillow. "I need to rest."

"Okay," Sue patted his arm. "Martha and I will come back later. We'll be here with you for a few days. We're both glad we were here to see you remember something from your past. Maybe this will open other doors for you soon. We missed you, Chad. Come back to us."

They gathered their things and left his room. Amy met them in the hall.

"Did he know you?" Amy asked them.

Martha shook her head, "Not us, but he remembered a horse we once had. Chad loved to ride it and he remembered it." Martha sounded hopeful. "You think he's on the way back?"

"Yes, I do. The therapist said he's getting images of the woods and machinery. He keeps seeing a skinny guy in the woods wearing an orange jacket." There was a question in Amy's voice. "Does any of that sound familiar to you?"

"They all wear those jackets. My brother-in-law, Gene insisted they wear bright orange so they don't get shot by deer hunters," Sue told her. "His foreman's name is Rusty, I know. He worked for years for Gene, then stayed on after Gene passed away."

"That could be useful. It's good you're here," said Amy. "I'm sure you're both going to help him a lot. Each time he recalls an incident, a scene, a face, even an odor, it will open doors to his past for him. I'm keeping a running log on all these incidents and I'll use them in the sessions I have with him by referring to names and places hoping to jog his memory. He still has some swelling in his brain, so the progress will be slow, but by keeping at events and associations, we can help him clear away some of the fog. Time will heal his wounds, but it's people like you two who will ultimately do him the most good."

Sue wiped her eye. "Chad is lucky to have such a dedicated doctor giving him so much time. I feel better knowing that he is in good hands."

Amy's cheeks began to glow pink. "You give me too much credit, Mrs. Wilson. I'm an intern here. I was rotated into emergency the night that Chad was brought in. It was the most frantic experience I ever had because there were three accidents that night and we were dreadfully short of help. Suddenly, Chad's case became mine, decisions and all. Believe me, I was a nervous wreck, hoping I wouldn't make a life-threatening mistake."

"Please, call us Martha and Sue. And as for what you did, to us it is nothing short of miraculous. We did go to the garage to see his car, you know. I'll dream about that for a long time to come." Martha put her arm around Sue. "We are always going to be grateful to you, Amy."

Chapter 41

The wedding ceremony touched Barry more than he thought it would. He was pleased to see his mother so elated. A whole new life was opening for her. In a few months she and Michael would be starting out fresh in Arizona. He'd miss her, of course, but it would be a great place to visit. He smiled to himself as he recaptured the glow on his mother's face during the ceremony.

The reception was at the *Coral Gardens* in northern Yonkers. He milled around the room that Mike had reserved for their guests, mostly Mike's family, some of his mom's neighbors and friends from work. Barry figured the crowd numbered about forty or so. He shook hands as he worked his way to the food table. On the way, he stopped at the bar and ordered a Jack Daniels, neat. He could sip at that for at least forty-five minutes. He felt alone, wished Amy could be here with him.

They ate, they danced and Barry had the time of his life. His mother introduced him to her best friend at medical records, Jenna Winger. Since their new insurance plan at St. Mary's Hospital, Jenna had maxofacial surgery on her teeth. She really did look like a model, like Fran had said.

Two Jack Daniels later, Barry was slurring his speech and telling his mom to have a rousing time in Nassau on that honeymoon. He even called his mom *ol' gal*. Fran looked over at Jenna and pointed at Barry behind his back.

Jenna came over and hugged Fran, "You go along and have a great time *ol' gal*, and I will be sure your son gets home safely." They both giggled. "I will not let him drive in this condition."

Jenna went over to the bar and sat next to Barry. The crowd was breaking up. "I came with a friend, but I'm driving you to Fran's house. May I have your keys, please?" She raised her palm up to his face.

He looked at her. "You're pretty beautiful," he slurred. "And pretty pretty. A real beauty. I think you're good looking, too."

"The keys?" She kept her hand outstretched. He reached into his jacket pocket and handed her the keys.

At the Kreitzler house, she helped him out of the car and up the three steps to Fran's front door. He stumbled awkwardly and leaned heavily against her almost taking her down.

"I'm taking your car with me. I'll get it back to you tomorrow. I'll be here early so you can drive me to work, okay?"

He grinned at her. "Aw, don't go. Come on in." He put his fingers to his lips. "Ssh. We can sneak in...oops, nobody's home. Come on, I'll show you my beddie room."

She followed him in. When he got to his bedroom, he sat on the edge of the single bed and seemed to melt down. Pushing him gently, he fell to the side. She lifted his legs to the bed and removed his shoes, struggled with his jacket, shirt and pants, covered him up and started to leave.

"I'll wait for you, doc. Hurry up." He muttered into the pillow.

"I only work in records, Barry." But he didn't hear her. He was snoring soundly.

"Next time it will be my place. I have a queen size bed." She stared down at him, pulled the covers up around his neck, pushed a stray strand of black hair back, then turned and left.

Jenna blew the horn early the next morning. Barry came out with a thermos cup of coffee and slid into the car next to her.

"I hate Mondays. You look great, Jenna."

"In a hurry. I'm almost late. I slept a little longer than I usually do." She backed out of the narrow driveway.

"Everything okay? Sorry about getting a little tipsy yesterday and thanks for driving me home. Was I…you know?" He blushed.

"Sure. You hit the bed snoring. Made me feel good, though. You called me 'doc' and I only work in medical records."

He was quiet. He sipped his coffee, Amy's face in his mind.

"Not a lowly job, Jen. I think 'doc' fits you." He looked over at her.

"Nah, it doesn't. You're too pretty to wear white all the time."

"That's what I call a super save. You're good, you know?"

"My mom's gone for a whole week. Want to do something? I have Wednesday and Friday afternoon off."

"What do you have in mind?" She shifted lanes quickly to get into the hospital parking garage.

"Want to go to Westchester with me? I found a great condo to sub-let. I'm meeting the real estate agent there. After I take a final look-see, we can dump her and have dinner. Sound okay? I feel I owe you for taking such good care of me last night."

"Sure, it would be nice. I did tell your mom I'd look after you." She looked over at him and smiled as she stopped in front of an elevator access door.

"Jenna, you're a year younger than I am. That's enough with the mothering already." He got out of the car and went around to the driver's side.

"I can go in early on Wednesday and be finished around three. Can you pick me up here?"

"See you then." He took over the wheel as she headed for the elevators. He watched her until she opened the door, looked back at him and waved.

Barry sighed. Jenna disappeared into the concrete and glass entrance of St. Mary's Hospital, but he was left with her lovely image. How many times had he heard his mom talk about Jen in medical records? He usually half listened to Fran prattle on about her work, the computers, Jen's frustrations with the arbitrariness of the programs and how they celebrated when they conquered the keys. All the little things Fran said popped into his mind now. He even remembered Fran talking about Jen's dental surgery. Focusing on his work in the D.A.'s office took precedence over all, but now, Jenna's face pushed everything out of his mind. Barry had his goals and they would never change, but he'd have to make room for Jenna Winger in his life.

Inside the glass doors of the hospital lobby, Jenna turned and watched Barry drive out of the lot. She pumped her fist into the air and whispered, "Yes."

Chapter 42

"I'm really tired, Dr. Crowley. Martha and Susan, they exhaust me."
He squinted at her. She stared back.

"You have incredible eyes, Chad. And call me Amy. I'm not really your doctor. Do you remember the girls telling you about your intense eyes?"

"No, I don't. I don't remember any girls including Martha, Shirley, and the girlfriend they told me about. And if you're not my doctor, why are you here?"

She leaned forward, "I want to be your girlfriend. I'm posing as a doctor so I can sneak in here and spend time with you, Bosley." She poked his arm.

"Yeah. Funny. Don't call me Bosley. My name is Chad…."

"Good. You know that for a fact?"

"It's what they tell me, anyway. I hate when you call me that other name. Chad's pretty cool. I don't mind being Chad." He winked at her.

Amy got up and walked to the window. It was very windy outside. The trees swayed, turning their leaves up to the sky. "What did Rusty call you?" She asked quickly.

"Boss. Always Boss. Well, I'll be. Where did that come from?" He looked amazed.

"Can you picture Rusty? What does he look like? Quick."

"Short, skinny and wrinkled, but he can spit tobacco juice at least fifteen feet. Amy, I can see him. Some of the men on the tractors, too. I can see a big chunk. My house, the evergreens, the big pond…Elk Pond…that's what they call the little township. I can see my car…Oh, God, I do remember. I sold the place. My head…I feel dizzy." He put a hand to the top of his head and leaned back.

"I need to write this up, Chad. You're doing fine. Repeat all this to the psychologist this afternoon, okay?"

He closed his eyes. "I guess I'll remember it all like everyone says I will, right?"

"Yes, you will. Just take your time and make sure you really remember on your own, not just what your aunt and cousin tell you."

"Amy, what did you mean when you said that you weren't my doctor?"

"I'm a resident here. I'm just interested in your case because it's fascinating and the experience is invaluable. You became a challenge to me even after I was rotated off the trauma ward."

"That's it?" He opened his eyes and looked at her. "I'm a guinea pig then? What a terrible letdown."

She leaned over him and placed her hand on his cheek, smiling into his fabulous eyes. "When I heard you were rich, I set my sights on you. I knew you were the one who could take me away from all this." She tweaked his nose.

"You're pretty funny, you know. When I'm all healed, I'll take you to lunch, okay? Money's no object."

"Like a date? A real date?" Her eyes went wide.

Over the next few weeks, Chad's memory came back in chunks. He even had flash backs of the accident. After he was bumped, he remembered flipping and slamming his head on the side of the door. The air bags inflated and then his world changed to blackness until he woke up in Room 702 in Massachusetts General Hospital. Martha and Sue helped toward filling in his once empty past but it was coming slowly and he was beginning to experience impatience and frustration.

Chapter 43

The plane was approaching LaGuardia. The attendant assisted passengers with seat belts. Maria fastened hers.

"Kyle, your seatbelt, sweetheart." She nudged him. "Honey, we're getting ready to land." She leaned her arm across his lap and scooped up the papers he had been studying on the flight.

Marie became aware of his shoulder slipping away from her. He continued his downward slip. He slumped sideways into the aisle. Marie screamed. "Kyle? What's wrong? Kyle?"

The attendant rushed to the intercom. "Is there any medical personnel on the airplane, please?" A young man rushed up the aisle and bent over Kyle.

"I'm an EMT and a registered nurse." He was a stocky man with a short goatee and moustache. He bent over Kyle, opened his shirt and felt for a neck pulse.

He looked up at the attendant. "Tell the pilot to delay landing until we can get him below. He's gone. Tell him to radio ahead for an ambulance."

Marie gasped. "Dead? No, he was sleeping. He was tired. Kyle's not dead. Check again please." Her disbelief was heart wrenching.

The EMT said, "I am so sorry. He is gone. Looks like a heart attack. I'll help get him ready for transport to the hospital morgue. He can be examined and pronounced dead there. Are you his wife?" he asked with compassion.

Marie leaned back against the seat. "How can Kyle be dead so fast? My God, what's happening here? This is all a mistake." She stared at Kyle sprawled in the aisle. Tears streamed down her cheeks. "Not his wife. Better. We were best friends."

She watched as he was gently placed on a narrow gurney, strapped into place and covered.

At the airport administrator's office, Marie was aware of a kind gentleman handing her an envelope. "These are Mr. Rodgers' belongings. You can pick up his luggage. Did he have a car in long-term parking?"

"Yes," she said softly. Her eyes were rimmed with red. "A black Jetta."

"We can drive you to the lot. Are you all right to drive?" he asked.

"Where is he? Right now, I mean?"

"At Medical Center East. Go to the lobby and ask for Dr. Evans. He'll help you. Do you want a driver?"

She began to shake. "I really don't know what to do. Can I use your phone?"

He slid the phone across the wide desk. She took a day planner out of her purse and turned to the list of phone numbers. She dialed the New York City Court House and asked for Barry Kretzler's extension. After a few moments, he came on the line.

"This is Barry Kretzler."

He was at the airport in forty-five minutes. He drove Marie to the hospital. She identified Kyle, told Barry all she knew about him and together, they decided to have his remains cremated. Since Marie knew of no relatives, Barry suggested she go ahead and drive his car back to State College, use his keys to go into his office and apartment and try to find names, addresses and phone numbers. He wanted her to fax these to him and he would handle the contacts. She agreed.

Chapter 44

"So what happens now?" Jenna sat on the sofa in Barry's condo. "What is she doing about his death?"

"I made her temporary executrix of his estate, whatever he has. There was no home, just a car, some valuable musical instruments and personal stuff. Marie found eighteen names, addresses and telephone numbers and I contacted them all. Not a relative in the bunch and none of them knew of any relatives either. So, she can sell what she wants, put the money in an escrow account and if no one comes forward within a reasonable length of time, then that's it. She's been at it for two months now. She needs to move on and I think she will. Working on two degrees leaves very little time to sit around and mope."

"It's so sad. To find someone to love and lose him so brutally. Sad." She pushed her long black hair back and sipped her brandy.

They both sat quietly, thinking of Marie and her unfortunate love affair.

Barry set down his drink. "So, what do you think of the new furniture? Classy, eh?" He swept his arm around the room.

She frowned, "Understated, masculine, but cozy. I love the chaise lounge, though. That was a stroke of genius, especially the placement by the French doors. The view of the gardens and the Hudson River is magical. I could sit here and sip brandy for hours."

"Sometime I sit there and study. I rest my eyes by looking out over the water. I even fall asleep there once in a while." He sat on the ottoman at the foot of the lounge. "Lean way back. Try it out. I'll rub your little feet."

Chapter 45

"We'll be taking him to the ranch until he's all healed. He's agreed to stay with us until he's out of the wheel chair." Martha spoke with Amy over coffee in the crowded hospital cafeteria. "He'll be fine with us. West Virginia in the late fall is a glorious place and winter will keep him settled by the fireplace. We promise to follow all the hospital directives and we will be in touch."

"I have all confidence in his recovery. He's strong and has an excellent skeletal system." Amy patted Martha's hand. "He has a good support system, too. He looked forward to your visits, you and Sue. You both have helped a lot already.

"He was always close with Mark as kids. When I married Mark, I inherited Chad. We became long-distance friends. His phone calls were always full of funny stories. He's just a great guy." Martha winked at Amy. "You went out of your way to help him, I know. We appreciate it. Without your interest in him he'd probably still be in a mist."

"He was easy to help. Plus, I learned a lot about that kind of trauma and its aftermath."

"Well, I better go. Dr. Cage said he'd sign him out around two. Mom's with him now. We'll gather his stuff and start back to Kensworth. Dr. Crowley, you're welcome to visit whenever you can get away. We have plenty of room and there's a lot to do in our area. I'll send some brochures to you. It's a great place just to relax, too. I'd love for you to come to visit. We feel we owe you so much."

"I appreciate the offer, Martha. It's pretty hard to plan getaways doing a residency like this. But, I'll keep it in mind and please, send the brochures, okay?"

She helped get Chad into the wheelchair. His left leg was in a boot, the cast was gone. His ribs were just about healed. Amy smiled, "You keep in touch now, Bosley." She leaned over and kissed his forehead. Chad smelled of after shave and masculinity. Amy looked at him softly, taking in his face, his shoulders, especially his incredible eyes.

"When I get healed, doc. Remember, when I get healed. Big date." He blinked his eyes at her. "Seriously, I owe you a lot, Amy. And I promise to call you with reports of my progress."

Martha wheeled him out of the room with Aunt Sue behind carrying a bag and a suitcase. Amy stood outside the door, hands in her lab coat pocket, watching their progress down the long hallway, the wheels making a soft swishing noise on the lacquered floor.

She stared at the now empty bed. A wave of loneliness swept over her. Aware of the intercom paging some doctor made her come out of her brief reverie. She sighed and headed for pediatrics.

Chapter 46

The phone in her apartment was ringing as she unlocked the door. She rushed to pick it up. Breathless, she gasped into the phone, "This is Dr. Crowley."

"I was about to hang up, Doc."

"Barry, what's new at the Court House?"

"My new job. I passed the bar in September. I am now Barry Kretzler, Esquire. That's right, baby. Esquire."

"Wow. You really are ahead of schedule. Tell me everything."

"Best of all, I've moved up to an office in the prosecutor's suite. No more grunt work in a cubicle. I have a real office and I'll be part of a team preparing cases for court. I'm heading in the right direction at last, Amy. I have my eye on assistant D.A. then D.A. for the city of New York."

"High goals, Mister. But if anyone can do it, you can. Congratulations, Barry. You did good." She chuckled.

"I thank our Foundation every day of my life. Without that scholarship I'd still be struggling to finish college, going nights and working."

"I hear you. How's your mother?"

"My Mom's in Arizona. She's a happy camper, traveling around the west with Michael. They sold the house in Yonkers. I'm in a condo in Westchester. I love it."

"Why didn't you just stay in your mom's house?" Amy asked.

"You know, I thought about it. But, I wouldn't have the time to maintain it. Here, I don't have a thing to do but enjoy the view." He sounded elated. She missed him, but she knew what he meant when he said he was busy. She didn't have time for much lately, either.

"How about you? Everything smooth and on schedule?"

"Getting close to my boards. Within the year I expect to be board certified and licensed. For now, it's internal medicine, then I'll look into a specialized field. The residency helps in making a decision since I'm involved in so many aspects of medicine."

"Oh, by the way, have you heard from Marie Maneros?"

"Not since her thyroid episode. Have you?" Amy sounded concerned.

He told her all he had done for Marie. When he finished, Amy was silent for a moment.

"Poor Marie. I was worried about her taking off with a university professor, but for other reasons. I never expected this."

"I know. It was a rough time for her. She went to Puerto Rico to be with her grandparents for a while, but she's back at school now. You ought to give her a call when you get a chance. Keep in touch with me, will you. I miss our breakfasts."

"I do too, Barry. Think we can pick up where we left off some day?" She laughed. She knew they couldn't but she wanted Barry to think that maybe one day they'd re-connect.

He hesitated. "The world is changing pretty fast now, but who knows."

"See you, Barry, and good luck." She smiled knowingly…Barry was gone. She hung up, turned to her empty apartment and headed for the shower.

Chapter 47

Michael Ridley called each of the five personally. The foundation money ran out at the end of the five years, final statements were sent out on time.

"She's in a wheel chair but she's very alert. She requests your presence on Saturday, June 11 at noon at the Lakeside Inn. Muriel Karetsky wants you to know that this will be the only time she would want you to come to Bluff View on her account."

All five agreed that no matter what was going on, they would be there. And they were.

Hal and Barry arrived Friday evening and went directly to the Romans' House. They sat on the sunporch watching TV and talking into the night.

"So the foundation has been good, Barry. I'm twenty four with a degree in engineering, a license in core sampling, another degree in metals and tensile measurements, and before long I'll have my own consulting firm. I'm working on environmental studies, too. I can work anywhere I please. I get offers from engineering firms all over the country. The company I work for bids on jobs from the east to the west coast. My family is relaxed because of their freedom of financial worries. Chuck is at Baylor on a football scholarship, doing pretty well, too. Hal sounded proud.

"Your sisters should be close to finishing high school now. They know what they want to do?" Barry looked out at the bright orange sun washing the piers in golden light.

"Typical teenagers, both of them. They have the energy, just lack the direction right now. I'm sure something will happen to get them focused."

"How's your love life?" Barry poured them second glasses of wine.

"Nada, pal. No time. Between projects, bids, on site experience, I barely have time for a TV show, let alone a date." He hesitated a moment, eyes distant. "There is a little dynamo at MIT in the architectural engineering program. She has real light blond hair, wide eyes, pouty lips, but a brain like Einstein. I did one project with her taking core samples on both sides of the Connecticut River for a potential bridge. She has the stamina of a tiger. I couldn't keep up with her. She mixed and poured concrete into the sample plugs, hefted equipment in and out of the pickup...I was extremely impressed. Did I mention she's a looker, too?"

"You did. Whatever turns you on. She sounds like she could play linebacker for the Packers." Barry giggled.

"All I can say is if I wanted to date someone it would be that little blondie. I would love to see her in a basic black dress with spiky heels. Bet she'd turn heads."

"Do me a favor when you get back. Ask her out. See if she even owns a dress." Barry shrugged. "Oh well, she might be a dynamo in whatever she's wearing, eh?"

Early Saturday morning, Sam, Marie and Amy arrived from the airport. Hal made pancakes and Barry poured coffees. There were hugs all around, everyone commiserated with Marie. They all chatted about school and their plans.

In a moment of silence Sam Carter said softly, "My Dad passed away last month. His life caught up with him, diabetes, heart, lungs."

They all expressed their condolences. He looked at Marie, "You would have been proud of me. At the church I sang his favorite song, one he sang to me when I was a child, one he sang softly when he was alone and in pain. And I sang it a capella, *Bye, Bye, Blackbird.*"

"I'm sure he heard it. I wrote a dirge for a friend of mine who passed away suddenly. The music department held a service for him. I played the music just for him and it was like he was right there next to me, listening, swaying to the music the way he always did." She reached over and clasped his hand.

Marie brightened. "On a lighter note, I just signed a one-year contract with a movie producer, *Blue Dreams.* I'm currently working on a score for a kiddie movie called *Hi-Kee-Na-Sun.* It's about a troublesome child in Hawaii who would rather surf than eat. Watch for it in your local theaters." She laughed.

Amy watched Marie closely. "You're finally out of the woods, aren't you? You're back on the track of carving out a career. You sound so confident."

Muriel's hair was silver, the long tresses twirled neatly into a twisted bun. Her blue eyes were as alert as ever. She still looked regal in a dark blue, long-sleeved, high-necked silk dress. She sat in her wheelchair at the head of the table, the view of the sparkling bay behind her. Her son, Edward Vincent was at her side as was Michael Ridley. Lisa oversaw the luncheon preparations, then joined the others at the table.

"I'll be brief," Muriel started. "Our experiment was a success, wasn't it? You all proved yourselves far beyond our expectations. Chet Romans and Pete Burkas, our dear friends, were right on target in their philosophy. Put the right people in the right place at the right time, provide the right conditions and the opportunities and it will all work out just fine. They lived by that code, right or wrong, they believed in it and thank God they did. I see five young people on their way to creating empires of their own. You all work hard, you're thrifty and no one abused privileges. Maybe when you're all finally settled in your careers you'll spend more time here at Bluff View." She paused and looked slowly around the table. "When I die, that will be the last of the original foundation board. We have new members, now, the next generation. Edward, Lisa, Michael, Jacqueline Kasinsky, Brian Harcher. We invite you to join the panel when you're established. Your scholarships are ending, the Romans/Burkas Foundation will get started on another set of five candidates. We welcome you to become a part of the process. Michael and Edward will keep you informed."

Edward Karetsky rose, kissed his mom on her forehead and handed each one a statement. He cleared his throat, "This is your latest foundation standing."

They all looked at their bottom lines which were very similar. They were all a little above or below three hundred and fifty thousand dollars. He continued, "As the elder statesman of the board, my mom wanted to have the pleasure of the board's final gesture to you. Mom."

Muriel gazed out the window then turned to the table. All faces were turned to her.

"I know money isn't everything, not the be all and end all of living. It doesn't even bring happiness, and it can't cure pain. But it's all we have, and here at Bluff View, we all respect its power. It gives the board pleasure to reward you for your sacrifices and hard work by adding a final gift of fifty-thousand dollars to each account. Now you can enter your various fields with ease. Good luck to you all." She suddenly looked very tired.

Hal said, "I don't know what to say. This has been quite an experience. You can certainly count on me to keep your wonderful work going on as long as I can."

"All my dreams of a sports medicine clinic can actually happen," Sam said wide-eyed. "I agree with Hal. I, too, would be proud to be a member of the foundation."

There were hugs all around. Lisa Karetsky wheeled her Mom out of the Lakeside Inn. A blue heron flew over the car as Lisa helped Muriel into the back seat. As Muriel settled in, she became aware of the bird perched on a piling at the end of the parking lot. Lisa backed out of the spot, turned to enter the road, as Muriel gazed at the long, graceful bird. She smiled.

Back inside, they finished their coffees, continued to chat and Marie leaned toward the table and whispered, "Does anyone know why the Harchers were not present?"

They all looked to Michael Ridley. His eyes were sad, his shoulders hunched. He picked up a napkin and toyed with the corner.

"It's not common knowledge but you should know that she has been institutionalized for depression, severe depression. No one knows why, but Brian thinks that the loss of two loves was just too much for her. Then the TV station let her go. They called it downsizing, but they did hire a younger anchorwoman. Her prognosis is fair, Brian says, but it will take some time. She's undergoing counseling and drug therapy. For a while, her only visitor will be Brian."

"An insidious disease. And it will take years of rehab, and even then, there is never a one-hundred percent recovery. Poor Jan." Amy shook her head thoughtfully.

Chapter 48

Everyone gathered their belongings and headed out to catch their flights. Sam Carter held back edging his way over to Michael Ridley and asking if he could see him privately for a few minutes.

"Sure, Sam. Edward and I are going back to the office. Ride along with me and we'll get you to the airport for your flight."

He sat across from Michael at the extra large mahogany desk. Sam cleared his throat and began, "I've been researching sites for a clinic. I'll be finished at UCLA in less than a year." Michael's eyebrows went up, he grinned widely. "I know," Sam went on, "I have no life. It's all cramming. But the late hours and the grind, it's all paying off. I'm ready for all the tests right now and I'm sure I'll ace them all. In the meantime, a classmate of mine wants me to go half on a sports rehab clinic in the Raleigh-Durham-Chapel Hill technology triangle."

"Good location, Sam. Is it an existing clinic?"

"No. It's a piece of land, two acres on Route 41, close to a hospital and could service suburban towns as well as the big three." Sam was tense, but excited.

"Okay, how much are you splitting?"

"We figured that for a half million we could build it and outfit it the way we'd like. With the time left on the scholarship, I'd like to transfer to Duke where I can finish and then go on to study orthopedic surgery."

"It sounds good, Sam. But you know we emphasize conservatism and caution. I'm not going to say yes until we do some research on this end to protect your investment. How much do you know about your partner? Can't be more than the years you've been at UCLA."

"Well, let's see, she's...."

"She?"

"Yes. Donna Worden. She's ready to take her exams, too. Her dad is Worden Construction of Winston-Salem. He'd be in charge of building. Cost of materials is all he's going to charge us. She's an only child, but not too pampered. After a few false starts, she's on the right page, bright and driven, just like me."

"And?" Michael squinted at Sam.

"Down the line a few years, I can see making her Mrs. Sam Carter. Is that what you mean?"

"Not exactly, Sam." Michael reddened. "But I will file away that information. What I meant was will she have the stamina and the tenacity to stick to a demanding practice?"

Sam lowered his eyes. "When I first started to talk with her, I would have answered your question with a firm 'no'. I suppose I was easy to talk to or something, because she confided so much to me. She's three years my senior, confessed to having an abortion after being raped the summer after she graduated high school. Her parents had her in counseling for the next year which helped, but she was reclusive. They finally convinced her to go to UCLA to get a teaching degree in science where she had excelled in high school. We met on campus and I talked her into auditing some of the medical classes."

"Orthopedics?" asked Michael.

"The medical machines, Michael. She was fascinated, couldn't get enough of those classes. I gave her Brian Harcher's number and they've been working on computer readouts and scanners and measuring devices. He's been to the school a number of times to work with her and the school bought into a number of their programs."

"Well, you do sound sure of yourself, and that's good. Give us a week and I'll get back to you, I promise," he rose and shook Sam's hand.

"I believe in this, Michael, and I don't think it's a frivolous request."

"I agree. Let us protect you for a little while longer though, okay?"

On the way to the airport, Michael looked over at Sam. He stared a moment then looked back out the front window.

"What?" asked Sam.

"Without sounding stupid…"

"Oh, yes. I didn't go crazy in college, if that's what you mean. Donna is an independent black woman. She's my kind of girl, Michael. You're going to love her." Sam laughed his deep throaty chuckle.

Chapter 49

Lost in reverie, Donna sat at the computer in the Duke lab. The new program from Harcher measured muscle strength and weakness. Donna applied it to the measurements of her recent patients and marveled at how it was able to transpose results to individual programs of rehabilitative machine exercises, lengths of time on each rep, vitamin and meds, dosages, massage and down times.

Long fascinated by resistances and weights, Donna worked hard to incorporate the technology into her application programs.

Her mind drifted to those almost forgotten years when she had no direction, no will, not even the stamina to go to school. Fortunately, her parents forced her to go to UCLA where she met Sam. Dear Sam. So gentle but so driven. He didn't have time for anything but his course of study, until he became interested in the lost little girl.

"Wake up, doc." A technician placed a pile of folders on the counter next to her computer. "You did my last group so well, my patients are responding beautifully. Could you apply some of that computer program to this group as well?"

"I will, but put the program on your inventory. It's real easy to use. Slide over here and I'll show you."

He rolled his chair over, leaned close to her and put his arm around the back of her chair, smiling at her mischievously.

"Uh, the program, sir. Just the program, okay?" She slid a legal pad to him. "Take some notes, sport."

"Okay. Gotcha." He blushed.

She scrolled the patients, their symptoms, background descriptions, current treatments and results.

Backing up to one name, Donna looked closer. Lori Ruiz, back injury as a result of an auto accident. It was a bruised coccyx, the prescribed treatment was fine, the prognosis positive.

"What about this one? Lori Ruiz. Is she responding?" Donna asked.

"Hmph," he snorted. "Real snot. Seventeen going on thirty. A real huffy Hispanic. Doesn't like the meds, the vitamins or the resistance machines. Doesn't like anything, really. Too young to be so bitchy, but she is."

Donna stared at the name, the address. It was Nino's sister. Nino was the boy who raped her, almost ruined her life. She felt strange looking at that last name, a name that came close to shutting her down completely.

"You all right, Dr. Worden?" the tech asked softly. "Do you know Lori Ruiz? Did I say something insensitive?"

"No, no. Nothing like that. I went to school with her brother, I think. That's all. Increase her reps and push the resistance up two notches. That'll keep her tired. Get rid of her faster, too."

Chapter 50

The architectural drawings of the proposed condominium complex at Gulfport Shores East were breathtaking. Hal took in the seven stories, the balconies, court yards, fountains, terraced roofs and elegant wrought iron trim. He turned the huge sheets to look at the structural frame. Bent low over the expansive drafting table, he was lost in thoughts of metal strengths, yards of concrete, the depth of the base, and myriads of other factors his chief engineer would have to consider before giving the builder the okay to go ahead.

The poke in his ribs startled him. She was smiling smugly up at him.

"Hey, Hal. You like what you see?"

"Michele? Michele Brooks? Long time, girl. What are you doing at Liberty Core?"

"Those are my plans you're picking over. What do you think? Pretty good, eh?" She was still hard as nails. He looked down at the name on the draft. Michele Brooks, sure enough.

"Yes, they are pretty neat. I was looking at these corners, though."

"What?" She leaned next to him. "What about them? They're up to code. Reinforced at every angle. What do you see?" She leaned over the draft and bent closer, frowning.

"Here. At the corners." He pointed. "The side supports look out of kilter. They're not positioned for high wind stress. Michele, did you go over this carefully? It's not how I remember your work at MIT."

"Oh, my God. They are out of position. But look." She put her brief case on the table and pulled out a folder stuffed with sheets. Spreading one on the table, they both scrutinized the careful drawings.

"Hal, here's my original draft. See, the struts are placed correctly. The building will stand hurricane force winds." She stared in disbelief at the draft.

"Maybe it's an honest mistake, but somewhere between your draft and this copy a terrible shift occurred. You getting credits for this job?"

"I am. Hal, could you make a mistake like that? The truth." She folded her arms across her chest and stared at him.

"I doubt it. Not on corners where there is so much stress. It wouldn't get far, though. Too many approvals it has to go through, you know that. But at this point you need to find out how and why it happened." Hal was sympathetic with Michele. "Go to your course consultant first. See what he says."

Michele decided to go straight to John Renner, president and CEO of Renner Architectural Designs, Inc. She didn't want one iota of doubt on her design no matter what the source.

John Renner was over six feet tall, iron gray hair, striking blue eyes, neat as a pin in a navy suit, light blue shirt and solid red tie. Michele noted how his posture accentuated his height. She smiled at him. She thought he looked like an I-beam, ramrod and solid.

"Michele Brooks, right?" He leaned over his glass-topped desk and shook her hand. "What can I help you with this morning?"

"I wonder if you could help me find out the reason for a glitch in my design for the condo project." She began to unroll the structural draft.

"Of course I will but, shouldn't you go to your course advisor? I usually see designs that are ready for approval. Don't get me wrong. I enjoy working with MIT grads because new ideas are the lifeblood of my company." He walked over to the drafting table where Michele was spreading the sheets.

"I didn't want my advisor in on this until I got to the bottom of how it happened first. Look at my design, then look at the plan done by your drafting department, especially here, at these northeast corners." She pointed to the changes.

John stared at the two designs intently. "This shouldn't have happened, Michele. Plans go through a lot of processes before final approval, but you're right. Leave these with me and I'll get to the bottom of it."

"I'm not leaving my originals, Mr. Renner. I'm too close to getting my second engineering degree. I don't need sabotage at this point. I came here to learn design because MIT listed your firm as outstanding and cooperative." Michele was red-faced and angry. She began to roll up the plans.

"Please, sit down. I promise you'll leave here completely at ease...."

"Mr. Renner, how can I be at ease when I'm looking at a gross error in transcription? Do you realize the damage that could occur at these joints during a storm? The only thing that could satisfy me is a conference with A.S., the draftsman who initialed this plan."

"Okay, I agree. I'd want to do the same thing if I were in your shoes." Renner was livid.

Michele rolled her original plan tightly and slipped it into her case. She sat in the oversized black leather chair across from John Renner.

"That was extremely bright of you, young lady. Too often our architectural designers don't bother to follow their plans that closely. Excellent work. We are a blue chip company of stellar designers, draftsmen and engineers. I would be honored to have you come aboard when you're ready, whenever you feel ready, that is. I could hire you today..."

"Let's not lose sight of how this error occurred." Michele was tight lipped and confused. Renner was trying to change the subject and it made her feel uncomfortable.

Renner slumped in his chair. "I've been in this business for 22 years. My company was never denied a permit. Never. Our structures won seven awards over the years, no small accomplishment in this field. We've built bridges of beauty and strength, three Las Vegas casinos, a cathedral and so on. Never a problem until now." His voice was low and shaky.

"Mr. Renner, what is it?" She was experiencing a feeling of anxiety.

"You used the correct word a moment ago when you said 'sabotage'. My sister's boy, Albert Spence came to work for me this past year. He finished drafting school and I promised his mom I'd give him an opportunity to work in our drafting department. He's a bit troublesome. His dad passed away when he was fifteen and he's been a little rebellious from time to time."

"And I just happened to be one of those times. Do you think he felt threatened by my internship here?"

"Probably. It's no excuse, though. He's reacted badly to students twice before. I hate to say it, but this time is strike three. I'm afraid I can't let him slide any longer. I'm sorry you had to experience this, but be assured that it is over. It just can't happen again."

"I don't know what to say. I hate to be in the middle of a family situation, but in all honesty, and with due respect, having him alter plans is a dangerous, malicious practice. Unsafe structures cost lives, Sir. You're carrying family responsibility way too far. I do appreciate your candor, though. Are you serious about hiring me on?"

"Dead serious. We have bids out on some exciting projects that will challenge your creative talents, imagination and vision." He came to life, his eyes shone. "A sea-quarium in Biloxi, Mississippi, a memorial bridge across the Susquehanna River in York, Pennsylvania, a modern art museum in Chicago, Illinois, to name a few. Are you interested?" He rose from his desk.

Michele was smiling. "Interested? Mr. Renner, I'm eager. It sounds like a fantastic opportunity. Can I get this engineering degree out of the way first? Say six to eight weeks more on my independent study, then the exam?"

Renner laughed. "I'll have a corner office for you in our Corporate Headquarters in Texas.

They shook hands again. "By the way," he straightened his tie. "The folks in Alabama are wild about the condo design. Your cleaned-up plans will be going to the builder in about two weeks."

"I appreciate that. I also appreciate the job offer." She gave him a thumbs up.

"Even though your home base will be Texas, you'll travel to

wherever we get the bids. You know how that works, right?" Renner's confidence was back.

Michele had an intelligent hunch that going to work for John Renner was the right move to make.

Chapter 51

The snow fell steadily through the night. It glistened in the trees under the lamplights and created soft mounds on bushes and tops of cars. Marie was restless. Standing by the window and watching the falling snow swirl around the streetlight outside her apartment made her recall Leipzig with its close, quaint buildings. She could hear the music in her mind, the music she and Kyle held hands to in the vast concert halls of Europe. Little gusts of wind sent loose snow skittering through the narrow street out front. Marie missed Kyle so much. He was the most supportive, unselfish man she ever knew. With Kyle, Marie and her education and her well-being always came first. Sighing softly, she let the curtain drop and recalled their last conversation on the plane about her finishing her masters and moving on. Then she remembered the card he gave her.

Marie dug into her purse and found Paul Andrews' card. She tapped it against her chin. With all this restlessness she was feeling, perhaps she was ready for a new direction. She dialed the second number on the card hoping it was his home phone number.

"Hello," a pleasant male voice answered.

"Paul Andrews?" Marie asked.

"Yes, this is Paul. Who is this please?"

"My name is Marie Maneros. I hope you don't mind my calling you at home. I'm a friend of Kyle Rodgers. He was my music mentor here at Penn State music department."

"Say no more, Ms. Maneros. I know you. Kyle told me all about you. He actually bragged about you, which Kyle never did."

"Well, he had only great things to say about your accomplishments, too. You were one of his favorite students, you know. He gave me your card right before he…."

"I know. In the world of music, he was a giant. He was a great teacher, extremely patient, wasn't he?"

"I know he was patient with me, Paul. We toured Europe for which I got credits, meanwhile, I fell hopelessly in love with him. I still haven't recovered from his passing. I miss him so much." She didn't want to sob over the phone talking with a man she didn't know, but the constriction was there.

"Were you with him when he died?" Paul asked gently.

"He died on the plane from London. I nudged him to fasten his seat belt and he slumped into the aisle. God, I haven't been able to talk about it for months, and now…." Marie choked.

"Hey, don't cry. I didn't mean to open up old wounds. It's just that I never heard any details. I was just curious. I'm sorry, Ms. Maneros."

"Please," Marie pulled herself together, "call me Marie. You know, you were the last person he spoke to me about before he put his head back to relax before the plane took off. The only reason I called you was because he gave me your card, told me about you and what you did and that when I got my degrees he suggested I call you. Well, I have all the degrees I need for now. I'd like to try something different."

"Look, I'm working on a documentary right now. It's a study of autistic children. Why don't you look at what I have so far and see if you'd like to try the score. I'll send you a tape of what we have. See what you can do with it, okay? We have a time line, though. Three months. Is that something you can handle?"

Marie thought of all the work she was capable of doing in three months. To her, it was a very long time, indeed.

"Send it, Paul. It sounds like something I'd like to work with. I appreciate the opportunity to work on something so intense. I look forward to it."

"All right, then. Is it snowing in State College? It's six o'clock here and I'm getting ready to take my steak and fries, and a beer, out on the deck and watch the sun go down in about two hours."

She laughed. "It's snowing pretty hard here. It's nine p.m. and I'm getting ready to go outside and shovel off my sidewalk to the street so I can get in my car in the morning. If it snows all night I'll have to shovel it again, but there will be less if I do it now."

"I do not miss the north. You have to come to California and work in our Beverly Hills studio. How would that be for a change of pace….and, no snow."

"Sounds wonderful. Let's see what I can do for you, first. You're sending me a challenge, but one I need right now. Actually, I can't wait to get started on it. It reminds me of the assignments Kyle used to give me from time to time, projects that were really meaningful and full of purpose. That's what this documentary sounds like to me."

She hung up the phone feeling a whole lot better. *Again, Kyle, I owe you,* she whispered into the night.

Marie shrugged into her coat, hat and scarf and went outside to shovel the soft, sparkling snow. It was easy to lift and toss off the sidewalk onto the piles already covering the lawn. The streetlight made the snow glisten and shine.

It's like shoveling diamonds and carelessly tossing them aside. These are all for you, Kyle, my love. Here's a big shovelful coming your way. Here's another, and another.

She shoveled feverishly, tossing the light snow as high as she could knowing that he was above, watching her, wishing her the best. She got to the end of the sidewalk, exhausted, and teary, but also elated.

I know your laughing at me, Kyle, but that's all right. I also know that these diamonds all around me as I rest on this shovel are an omen of what's to come and it's all because of you, because you led me to Paul Andrews and he's the challenge I need right now. Rest easy, Professor, your star pupil is about to make you proud.

Chapter 52

Edward Vincent Karetsky sat across the booth from Donna Worden, their lunches in front of them. Edward was a striking business type in a well-fitting grey suit, striped tie, smoothed back wavy black hair, tan with even, white teeth. He put Donna at ease with his relaxed manner.

Donna picked at her salad. She was a slim girl with an athletic figure. Her eyes were almond-shaped and a deep, rich brown. Donna's skin was pure mocha, a model's coffee and cream complexion. She wore her hair close-cropped, shiny and curly. Hoop earrings made her look confident. This was a no-nonsense girl and Edward appreciated everything about her.

"Are you an equal partner with Ridley, or are you the second string?"

He laughed. "I am a full partner, Donna. I hope you understand the reason for my visit with you."

"Sure. Sam is about to invest a lot of money and Ridley Associates is like his big brother or something so you need to check me out to be sure I'm not some kind of flake who might run off with Sam's money. Am I right?" She sipped her diet coke.

"We just like to get a feel for a big expenditure. We have kept tabs on all the foundation money spending. That's why all five candidates are finishing with more than the amount that was put in their individual accounts initially. Michael Ridley's conditions are protective, not abusive. This is a big step that Sam is taking. We just want to be sure that the both of you are on the same page." He nodded at her. "When it comes to money, the Ridleys go way back to the turn of the century and, proudly, never had a client file for bankruptcy, even through the depressions and recessions. I suppose you might say that the firm is the most disciplined in the field."

"I see. But, Edward, notice that my father, who is financing my half of this venture is not sending the financial police to investigate Sam."

"I'm not investigating you, either. Understand that I'm merely trying to get a feel for you and Sam and what you're attempting. I think it's admirable, and, down the line, will be profitable...."

"But you boys in Chicago need to have control...."

"It's the kind of control that works, though. Money without discipline can only lead to disaster. We have been extremely successful managing people's finances and yes, we are disciplined and have our conditions, but if there is compliance, historically, there will be profits."

Donna lowered her eyes. "I do understand positive control. I rebelled against it at one time. It was only when I surrendered myself to the guidance of others was I able to move forward, become self-disciplined, and make up ground I had lost. So I know where you're coming from. I just like to press the buttons once in a while to see how people react. You're good. You're steadfast."

"That's me. Good old solid Edward Vincent." He bent his head over and smiled at her. "If I were twenty years younger, not happily married and a proud father...well, who knows. You're a very pretty woman, Donna Worden, and sharp as nails."

"I appreciate those words and take them as a compliment. I'll be marrying Sam Carter in the future. He doesn't know that yet, but you'll be at our wedding, Edward Vincent."

He prepared Donna for some intrusion in the pre-building process. He explained Hal Jensen's role in establishing core sampling at the site for a building that would house heavy equipment. He also told her that Barry Kretzler would be drawing up some legal papers to protect both sides.

"We just wouldn't want Sam's investment hanging out there all by itself if for some reason you decide to default."

"Do what you must. I'm sure my father will agree to whatever I tell him. He just wants to build the clinic. We insist on paying him because he's the best builder around with strong references. I'll mail you a copy of those as soon as I get them together. His business is 'Frank Worden Construction.' I'm ready to start the facility while Sam continues his studies. He'll work with me part-time. I don't want him to delay his orthopedic surgery degree, and Duke is a great school for him to finish. He's brilliant, you know."

"We have no doubt he will be an excellent surgeon given his drive and determination. Well, my dear, let me get my notes together and we'll get back to you. Hal will go to the site by the end of the week and get back to us with his results over the weekend. Then Barry can do his thing. We should be ready to release Sam's money shortly after that." Edward got up to leave.

"Are you staying somewhere here in L.A. tonight? If so, have dinner with Sam and me."

Edward hesitated. "He doesn't know I'm here. We kind of decided that this visit was sensitive, for both of you. But, it's your call. The Sheraton has a very nice dining room. Talk to Sam. If he agrees, I'll be there at six. I have to eat anyway. The company would be nice."

"We will be there." She rose and shook his hand. "Uh, your treat, right?"

He laughed out loud. "You learn fast. My treat."

Chapter 53

"Thanks for bringin' the bail bond, boys. I appreciate it. Stupid cop. Caught me liftin' one of them gold chains off the rack. Pah! It was junk anyway." Ivan Kutos sneered out the back seat window. "I don't know how he picked up on it. I palmed it neat. Guess he had a good view."

"You the stupid one," Craig Machlich said. Maybe you're getting' too old, losin' your touch."

"Boss is gonna be pissed. He don't like no attention like that." Jerry Appleby shook his head.

"Hey," Ivan piped from the back seat. "I saw somethin' pretty interestin' at that precinct. Maybe the boss won't be so pissed when I tell him who was there."

"Yeah? Who?" Jerry wanted to know.

"That friend of Margie, Hank Kershaw. That guy who does all that pimpin' and the smart movin'. You know who I mean." Ivan was excited.

"What was he doin' there?" Jerry was curious.

"He's a little weasel. I had a couple run-ins with that one. Cocky. Smart ass. And he's at the cop shop? What'd you see?" Craig drove a little faster.

"Take it easy," Ivan lowered his tone. Craig was all agitated. "For one thing, he could have been payin' a speedin' fine or somethin' like that, but, he was on the wrong side of the counter standin' way back with two tecs."

159

"You sure it was him? Maybe it was someone looked like him. You know, there's a lot of small, skinny guys with glasses," Jerry said, frowning.

"Nah, it was him. He turned three or four times while I was talkin' to these two guys. I got a good look."

"Son of a bitch. Bet he's a narc. He's watchin' us for some reason. Givin' us enough rope, then…Bam…we all get rounded up." Craig was red-faced.

"Why don't we watch him for a while. You know, be sure, then serve him up on a platter to the boss. Could be a fat pay check, eh, Craig?" Jerry laughed a deep, hollow, distorted bray.

"Hey, don't forget about me, guys. If it wasn't for me, we'd never know about the narc, right?" Ivan sounded worried.

"Yeah, yeah. But for now, you shut up about it. Just go about your business and keep quiet."

"But what about the boss? He's gonna be mad at me. Can't I tell just him?"

"No," Craig raised his voice. "We'll handle this. Just continue bein' the payroll clerk and deliver the pay-offs like you been doin'. We'll handle the boss, you hear?"

"Okay, okay," Ivan said nervously. He was sorry he ever said anything to these two nuts. He was sorry he had such a big mouth.

Two nights later Ivan was on the Shore Road in Bay Ridge heading for the Corsican Club. He had to deliver two envelopes, but first he checked the little card that he took out of his wallet. It contained names and amounts. After checking off two names, he headed for the front door where he noticed a group of smokers hanging around. Glancing around, he noticed Hank Kershaw and Little Margie against the building. Hank was pressing her pretty tightly against the bricks. She was giggling.

"Well, well, well. What do we have here? Kind of out of your turf, aren't you? Hello, Margie. Slummin'?" Ivan sauntered over, pulling himself up straight, all-knowing.

"Hit the road, Kutos. Unless you got a fat envelope for me." Hank sneered at Ivan.

"Real big shot, aren't ya?" Ivan whispered. "Well, I'd watch my ass if I were you, ya little weasel. Think you're so smart all the time. I'd find a different boy toy if I was you, Margie. You got your brains up your ass these days." He turned and went into the bar.

"Margie, wait in the car. I think Kutos has a pretty big mouth. I'm gonna have a little chat with him." He handed her the keys.

Ivan came out of the car, lit a cigarette and walked slowly to his car. He inserted the key, opened the door and Hank Kershaw was all over him. He pushed Ivan in and slid in beside him pushing Ivan to the passenger side.

"What the hell are you doin' ya piece of crap. Get outta my car," Ivan shouted.

"Put your seat belt on, we're taking a little ride." Hank peeled out of the parking lot, headed up Bay Ridge Road to Shore Drive, made a right and sped toward the bridge. Ivan made a move to his inside jacket pocket. Hank hit the brakes hard. Cars behind him swerved, brakes squealed and Ivan flew against the dash, hard.

"Told you to use your seat belt, jerk off." He reached over and took the wallet from a dazed Ivan's pocket. Horns sounded angrily as Hank pulled back into traffic.

"Where...where are you going?" Ivan had a handkerchief over his bleeding lip.

"We're going where you can chat with some people. It's all over for you, Ivan. Now we'll see what kind of a deal we can cut for you." He turned into the parking lot of Manhattan South Precinct Headquarters.

"I knew it. I knew you was a narc. I was right. Well you won't be so smart for long, ass hole."

"See, Ivan. You keep saying things like that. That's what we need to clear up. Who have you been talking to and what have you been saying?" Hank cuffed Ivan to the steering wheel.

"You stay put. I'll send someone out to read you your rights. If you're a good boy, maybe they'll cut your prison time a little bit."

He sat on one side of the window and watched and listened to a very not-so-cocky Ivan tell the interrogator how Hank's cover was blown.

"So they told me to clam up. Jerry and Craig. They're two mean guys. I'm sort of afraid of them, they're like crazy, y'know? They said they'd take care of Hank…and they will. I know those two. They done this before. Craig carries a Colt revolver and Jerry loves his Ruger. Craig's gun has a white handle with an eagle on it. Pretty nice. He's always showing it off."

The questioning officer intimidated Ivan to the point where he turned completely over on everyone he knew. He warned them about Jerry and Craig. He said he was deathly afraid of them, again. He agreed to testify against all of them but he wanted protection, foolproof protection.

Chapter 54

Hank drove Ivan's car back to the Corsican, noticed that his car was not in the lot. He went up to one of the guys hanging around out front.

"Where's Margie?" he asked.

"Those two head cases, Machlich and Appleby took her and your car. They said they'd meet you at the Starlight Motel on Bay Ridge Drive. Said they wanted to talk."

"How about a ride over there, Bennie?"

"Sure. Not doin' anything. I'll go around back and get the car. Gimme a minute."

"Wait for me," Hank headed for the bar door. "I need to make a quick call."

The D.A. shouted into the phone, "Do not go to that motel alone, Hank. You wait for backup. Barry and I will be there as soon as we can. I need to call the chief. Don't do this by yourself. That's what they want, that's how they operate. They get you alone and then they'll ambush you. Park down the street and wait, you hear?"

"Yeah, yeah. Just hurry up, okay?" He hung up and headed out to the waiting Bennie. "But what about Margie?" he muttered. "They have Margie now and it's my fault. Someone needs to help her fast and it's going to be me."

Hank got out of Bennie's car. He saw his parked in front of Unit 22. "Thanks, Bennie. See you around." Bennie took off. In the far distance he could hear sirens. His backup.

"Margie?" he called out. There was no answer. He turned the knob and the door opened. He knew immediately it was a setup. It was too easy to get in. Where the hell were they? He slipped back out, looked left and right along the covered concrete walkway. No one. He took out his Remington, pushed the door hard. It banged against the wall. He didn't move. It was dim inside but by the soft light of a corner lamp he could make out Margie tied spread eagled to the bed, naked, bruised, bloodied. She was alone, her mouth was taped shut.

He went all the way in swinging his gun left and right, kicking open the bathroom door…empty. He went over to the bed.

"Aw, Margie, Honey. I'm sorry. Jesus." He untied her hands and legs and pulled the tape from her mouth.

"We have to go," she choked. "They'll be back, come on." She grabbed at her clothes from the floor as Jerry and Craig came through the door, their guns pointed at Margie and Hank. The sirens were growing louder. Hank raised his gun and fired low. They returned fire as Margie jumped in front of Hank, screaming, "No. Don't shoot."

Margie slumped, blood gushing from her stomach. Behind her, Hank fell forward against her. "Oh," he was surprised as the bullet ripped through his side.

Craig fired once more as he ran out the door following Jerry. The sirens were all around the motel. Bright lights, blue and red, caught the fleeing gunmen, Craig limping, his right thigh spewing blood.

Chapter 55

The arraignment was set for the next day. Barry and the D.A. were pushing for the death penalty. The men were charged with the attempted murder of Detective Henry Kenshaw, the murder of Margaret Hurley, drug trafficking, extortion and loan sharking. An eyewitness revealed three other murders allegedly committed by Craig Appleby and Jerry Machlich. An ongoing investigation resulting in the exhumation of the bodies could lead to further charges.

Barry Kretzler, A.D.A. of New York City stood outside the cells of the two men. Craig's leg was in a cast. Both men sat on their cots looking sullen.

"Well, boys. Looks like we got the whole mess of your buddies in crime. But you two are the first prize. You two make it all worth while."

Jerry looked up. "You some kind of big shot lookin' to make a deal?"

"No. Not today. I could make a deal, I could recommend clemency, all kinds of good stuff like that. I could recommend that you get counseling because of your lousy upbringing, your ridiculous mental state, extenuating circumstances. I'm in a position to offer you numerous options. But, too bad for you, I don't have to, I don't need to, I especially don't want to. We have a witness who sang like a lark. The Bay Bridge area is finally free of you two cockroaches."

"That rat bastard, Ivan. He's a dead man, he is," Craig shouted.

"Now you're threatening a witness. A gem of a witness, too. Not very bright, though. He was carrying a list with him, a payroll, can you imagine that?" Barry paced in front of the cells.

"You made a deal with him?" Jerry asked.

"A sweetheart deal. That dumb Russian will be laughing up his sleeve for the rest of his sorry life, while you two, well, what can I say. If we find just one bullet in those bodies that match your guns, well, that will nail you with the death penalty for sure. As it is, even without the forensic evidence, I'll be pushing for lethal injection for the murder of Margaret Hurley and the attempted murder of Detective Kenshaw."

"Too bad we didn't get that narc bastard, too." Jerry stuck out his chin.

Barry stared at the two. He leaned on the bars of their cells, looking at them quietly for a moment. "You know, it doesn't matter why you're going to die. For me, you're dying for a murder you committed ten years ago at a subway station in lower Manhattan. My father, Frank Kretzler was on his way home from work when you two jumped him, robbed him and pushed him down onto the tracks. After a week in the hospital, he died. I went to your hearing. You got off. I told you then that someday you'd pay for what you did to my Dad. It took ten years and now I'm in a position to see that, finally, you pay. Your lawyer at that time told me to go home, that it was all over. That's what I'm going to do now. I'll file my brief then walk away from you two scum bags. But know this for sure. For you, it's all over. As the attorney of the deceased Frank Kretzler, I'm assuring you, boys, it's all over."

"I don't even remember your old man. You sound like the one who's a nut case here. Who cares what happened ten years ago? No one remembers, no one cares." Jerry's voice rose, a note of fear finally rising through the bravado.

As Barry started down the hallway he turned and said, "I believe you'll remember Frank Kretzler when the poison is coursing through your veins. I just hope it's slow enough so you have time to remember all your victims."

Craig shouted after him, "We can give you names. We can deal, we'll turn over."

Barry shouted back, "There's no one left, boys. Your buddy, Ivan sang an aria that shook the halls of justice. You have nothing, no one. You're all alone and you'll die alone. I'll see to it. I'll see that you die within an hour of each other. Play cards to see who goes first, assholes."

Barry went back to the court house and took Detective Matt Harrison's card out of his desk.

"Hello," Matt said.

"Detective Harrison? This is Barry Kretzler."

"I know, Barry. I heard through the grapevine. Congratulations."

"Thanks. I'll be throwing your folders into the mix, too. I owe you, Detective. Can I buy you dinner?" asked Barry.

"Sounds good. Right after the sentencing. You've come a long way, young man. I'm glad I'm still around to see justice finally being done. Feels good, doesn't it?"

"It sure does, detective. Even though it took a long time, it feels real sweet."

Chapter 56

After Marie got her masters in Performing Arts, she had dinner with two of her close classmates and the head of the music department. Professor Phil Layton admired and respected Marie's talent, and had, in his desk drawer, a letter of recommendation from Kyle Rodgers. He asked her to stay on and teach at Penn State. She sat over dessert and reflected on what had brought her to this point in her life, the death of her parents, the hard work, the foundation, Kyle, the passing of both grandparents in Puerto Rico. She was wealthy but lonely. There was her music, her brilliant music, but there was an emptiness in her that even composing, arranging and transcribing couldn't fill.

"I'm going away for a while, Professor Layton, but I'll be back for orientation and scheduling. I appreciate your offer and I accept. I'd be honored to be a part of the music department staff," she told him.

She spent a week at Romans' House in Bluff View before her duties at Penn State began. Hosting a party for the neighbors gave her a chance to renew old friendships with the Ridleys, the Karetskys, the Harchers, a few newcomers. Lisa insisted on catering from the Lakeside Inn. It was cozy, relaxing and fun. She walked the beach, did some shopping and left feeling renewed and ready to tackle her new challenges.

There were a half dozen messages on her answering machine from Paul Andrews. She dialed his number.

"Hello, Paul. It's Marie. I've been away. I got your messages."

"Then you know I loved your score for *Morning's Children*. You

168

nailed it. It's sensitive, inspirational, and you've tied it all together beautifully. The theme song *Out of the Mist* blew me away. Blue Dreams Studio will use your score, Marie. All of it. Come to New York so we can get going on our next project. What do you say?" Paul was excited.

"I can't, Paul. I start teaching in less than two weeks. You're talking to Professor Marie Maneros, now."

"We can work something out. Teachers get a lot of time off during a year, right? And you won't be working half as hard teaching as when you were studying. There will be holidays, breaks, summers and semester gaps. Can we try it? I really want you to continue writing music for us. Sign our contract so we can begin. A lot of it can be done at home like you just did. But it would be better if you could do some work here at the studio. I realize California would be difficult, but New York isn't that far from State College. What do you say?"

Marie was tempted. "Sounds like I'd be doubling my work load, Paul, but maybe that's just what I need. Can you send me a copy of your contract? I'll look it over and decide what to do. How does that sound?"

"Sounds fine. Let your lawyer look it over, make changes if you like. Let's just do it Marie." Paul had a child like quality in his voice that made Marie feel comfortable. Almost the same feeling she had when she first met Kyle.

"Does Blue Dreams have a fax machine, Paul?" she asked. "We have one here in the business office. I could fax it to you. Would that work?"

"Yes. Good idea. I'll fax it to you this afternoon. But don't return it for at least five days. I have to go to our San Diego studio. I'll be back here next Wednesday. Is that okay?"

Marie agreed. "Do you do that very often, go back and forth between the studios? How many are there, anyway?"

"New York, San Diego, Beverly Hills, Tampa and a few shooting locations that we own. I was exclusively in the San Diego studio until I got promoted to Production Manager which gave me responsibilities on both coasts, so yes, I do a lot of flying, at least ten or twelve times a year." There was that appealing tone in his voice again.

Marie laughed. "You're a real jet-setter."

That afternoon, as promised, Marie got the three-page contract from Paul. She picked up the phone and called Barry.

"Do you have a fax machine and the time to look at a three-page contract?" she asked.

"For you, there's always time. We have one in administration. Let me get you the number. What's up?"

"I guess I'm going into show business." She explained the contract and her problems with time. "I can't get into a contract that would interfere with my teaching duties, so see if this could work for me, okay?"

"Well, we can make sure that it doesn't bind you to them too much." He gave her the number.

"Everything going well with you, Barry?"

"So far, things couldn't be better. I'm happy in my work and there is so much room here for promotion. It's a promising future. You?" he asked gently.

"Getting a position in the music department here was a giant step, but this other thing, show business, writing scores for documentaries, sounds like where my talents lie. So I've been told. But, I want to take it slowly, to be sure."

"I heard from Amy about your grandparents. I am so sorry. They were so proud of you. You must miss them terribly," he said.

"You know, Barry, it was so fast it was almost a blessing. I flew to Puerto Rico because my Grandma got sick. On my way there, she passed away, and two days after the funeral my Grandfather had a heart attack and joined her. I'm glad that I agreed to stay with him for the week after the funeral. So, they are both buried in the beautiful San Juan that they loved." Marie sighed.

Chapter 57

Winter break at Penn State started in mid December and lasted until the second week in January. Marie had two students who were going to be out until the middle of March and ten who were on Independent Study. Paul's call was just what she needed to shake her out of the winter doldrums.

"Guess what? The score of *Morning's Children* has been nominated for a Golden Globe. Congratulations, Marie. Kyle said you could do it and when I heard it I knew it was a winner. Can you come out and go to the awards with me?"

She was eager to fly to California to meet him. "At last I get to put a face to the voice. I have a lot of time on my hands so, yes, I will be delighted to attend."

"I hope you're not too disappointed. Kyle told me all about you, so I guess I'm a step ahead. Look, I'll meet you at the airport, main entrance. I'll be wearing a white sport jacket with a red rose in the lapel. You won't miss me."

She dragged her bag across the concourse, her open raincoat flapping around her. Marie looked beautiful, makeup flawless, hair short, loose and curly, a look of curious anticipation in her eyes. She walked briskly through the open glass doors searching the crowd milling around in front seeking connections with loved ones. Cabs were lined up, drivers carried placards with printed names, others shouted out names to the passersby.

Marie stopped in her tracks. Others walked around her. She threw her head back and laughed out loud.

"Very clever. Paul, I presume?" She had a hard time holding back a choke.

Paul stood against a column. He was well over six feet tall, built square, an angular, solid face, jet black hair that was curly and super shiny. Marie's first impression was, handsome. In his white lapel he wore a single red rose, long stem, leaves and all.

"I didn't want you to miss me." He looked at her approvingly. "Now, I don't want to move. I want the moment to last."

Marie smiled. He took her bag. "May I have the rose? You know, to make the moment last? I'll press it in the pages of my song book."

He removed the rose and handed it to her. She grinned as she walked by his side. Marie felt like she was home, at last.

Chapter 58

The afternoon was hot. Donna was a little afraid to slip down the embankment to join Hal, Michele and Frank Worden. Her Dad was pointing at something at the back of the lot. The three of them got into Hal's pick-up and drove through the tall grass. Hal began chopping at the weeds. She knew that he would make a hole, sink an instrument, mix up some concrete and pour it into the hole to make a core sample to take back to his lab. She hoped the high North Carolina water table would not be a problem.

She marveled at the help they were getting from the foundation and how much Sam's friends were willing to pitch in. Leaning against the car, she watched traffic patterns. It was a busy stretch of road with connections to the tri-cities. Good location, Sam was convinced..

A tan pick-up with a loud motor pulled ahead of her car leaving a trail of shoulder dust. A pouty Hispanic young man got out, left the door open and sauntered over to Donna.

"Hey, sweet thing. Remember Nino? How you been? Thought that was you. I just had to stop to say hello." He wore tight jeans and an open, yellow shirt. Two gold chains hung against his tan chest, a gold hoop in each ear.

"Best thing you can do is get back in the truck and move along." Donna was tense, arms folded tightly against her body. "I never turned you in, Nino but I should have. Should have let your parents in on some of the mess you made."

173

"Ah, c'mon, Donna. We had a pretty good thing until you got snotty on me. I just brought you down a peg, is all. No harm, right?" He stared at her with flashing eyes.

"Please go. I'm not down a peg any more and I certainly don't want to sink to your level again. Those days are gone forever. Keep your distance and everything will be fine. Start bothering me again and you'll be very, very sorry. I promise you that." Her eyes were wide with false bravado, but she had to be strong.

"What you doin' here along the road anyway? You with those people out there? What's going on?" He stared across the field.

"Not your business. Get in your car and go. I don't want to see you again, ever."

"Well maybe those folks would like to know about you and me. I hear from some people you're a big shot doctor and all now. Maybe I think about five grand will keep me quiet, eh? What do you think, baby? Worth it to keep my yapper shut?"

Donna saw Sam's car approaching, blinker flashing, easing off the road. She looked at Nino and said, "Meet me at Rosewood Mall tonight at 9. Near the far end. Now go."

Nino got in his truck, waved and merged into traffic.

"Who was that?" Sam asked as he came to stand next to Donna. He shaded his eyes and watched the little tan truck weave in and out of traffic.

She hesitated only a moment. "I was going to tell you he was just asking for directions, but…" her voice trailed off, eyes tearing.

"What is it? Come here," he wrapped his arms around her tightly. "That was the guy, wasn't it? The one who hurt you. What did he want?"

Through choking sobs she blurted out, "Yes, that was Nino. He wants money now, to be quiet. I'm messing everything up all over again."

"No, no you're not. Because now you're not alone." Sam put up his arm and waved Hal, Michele and Frank over. They climbed down the embankment and met the truck in the middle of their lot.

When Donna finished telling them what had happened, Hal reached back for his cell phone and dialed Barry Kretzler.

Chapter 59

At nine sharp Donna was in place. Many of the mall stores were closing, the parking lot was thinning out. There were three or four cars scattered in the far corner of the lot when she pulled in against a grassy strip. She put out the lights, shut off the engine and waited in the dark, fingering the envelope.

He drove to the far end of the lot and noisily pulled in beside Donna's car angling so she wouldn't be able to back out. Nino slid in beside her.

"Nice going, girl. Got the dough?"

She took a large white envelope out of her purse and threw it onto Nino's lap.

"Hey, no need to be mad. We can be friends, like we were, you know." His hand went to her knee. She cringed.

"Come on. For old time's sake. What do you say? You're sweet, I'm hot, let's get it on."

The door flung open and strong arms pulled a surprised Nino from the front seat. The police officer grabbed the envelope and pushed Nino against the trunk.

"You know the drill, pal." Two police cars pulled up, lights twirling. Sam got out of one of the cars that was parked in the dark and slid in next to Donna. "You all right, Hon?"

She stared straight ahead. "I'm so ashamed to put you and my Dad through this. Not to mention Hal and Michele. It's like the past is an albatross around my neck. I'm so sorry."

Frank climbed into the back seat. "No need to be sorry. You did nothing wrong. But Nino, there, he did everything wrong. His folks will make bail tonight but, believe me, he will be convicted and sentenced. The past is catching up with him, thanks to you."

Hal and Michele watched as one of the police officers read Nino his rights. He looked over at the couple. "What the hell you lookin' at?"

"I'm not sure what it is, but it's the lowest form of scum of some kind." Hal smiled at Nino as the officer pushed his head down into the back seat of the patrol car.

The arresting officer told them that Nino would be arraigned, his parents called, a lawyer would get involved, bail would be set, but Nino would eventually end up in jail thanks to the conversation he had with the ADA of New York.

"I was a good witness. You folks had some good advice. Nice job."

Nino worked in a battery factory three miles out of town. He stopped at a convenience store just after one a.m. after his middle shift was over. He came out with a small bag and headed for his car. As he got in, he was pushed roughly over to the passenger side by Frank Worden. Hal squeezed him to the center as he slid in from the passenger side. Sam had himself tucked into the tiny back space.

"What...what's going on?" he asked angrily.

"Just going for a little ride with you, that's all." Frank looked straight ahead as he drove the pick-up back out of Durham.

He turned off the highway onto a dirt road, a construction site. There were boards, buckets, a half-framed structure, all surrounded by a heavily wooded area.

Hal pulled Nino out of the truck. "You got away with a lot in your miserable life. Now, you found three crazy guys who love this kind of stuff." He tied Nino's hands behind his back.

Frank led them to a wide plank. It looked almost white in the moonlight.

"You're all getting into a lot of trouble, you know. You can't get away with this nonsense." Nino was close to tears.

"Sure we can," Sam soothed him. "You did, didn't you?"

Frank tied Nino's legs spread-eagled to the plank. He leaned over Nino and said, "You did dirt to my daughter."

Sam said, "To my fiancée."

Hal said, "My friend." He pulled the snap open on Nino's pants and pulled the zipper down.

Frank came up close to Nino with a chain saw, pulling at the start cord. It made a whirring noise in the night. Two white birds exploded out of the dark pines.

"Oh, God, no. You can't. I'll bleed to death. Please, I'm sorry, so sorry. Untie me, let me go. Please. No more." Nino squirmed frantically against the ropes and the noise of the saw.

Frank stopped the saw. Nino had wet himself, a dark stain in the moonlight. He sobbed softly.

"You do your time, you hear?" Frank whispered. "And when you come out, the Wordens and all good people are off limits, understand? You're going to be a fine citizen from now on. If not," he held up the saw and smiled wildly in the bright moonlight showing white, shiny teeth. "Remember, there are three crazy guys out here, just layin' for you."

"And not just for you, creep. We'll plant drugs on your family and call our buddies at the police station. Don't even think of jay walking. Keep your shoplifting sister off the streets, too. You need to be a straight arrow. No more shit." Hal smiled. Sam laughed his throaty, deep rumble as he untied a shaking Nino.

After Nino sped down the dirt road to the highway, the three of them laughed uproariously.

Frank choked, "I think he might find Jesus."

"Whatever. I'm sure he won't be bothering anyone any more," Sam said.

Hal spoke through convulsive yuks, "He's going to be afraid to take it out to piss."

"Good."

Chapter 60

Amy sat in her office at Mass. Gen. poring over a case file and having a cup of coffee. Rounds always tired her out. The phone on her desk buzzed.

"Dr. Crowley, this is Connie at the front desk. There's a gentleman here to see you. He said his name is Bosley. You want him to come up?"

"No, tell him I'll be right there," she answered with a laugh. She locked her office door and took the stairs the two flights down.

He sat on one of the benches in the waiting area, holding a cane at his side. Her heart skipped a beat, Chad was so good looking. She felt lucky to know a man like him.

"I didn't know you were coming to town? Did you fly in? Why didn't you tell me you were coming?" She hugged him as he stood up.

"I wanted to surprise you. Do you have time?" He held her tightly.

"I have an appointment at two, then, I'm free for the weekend. I'm a real doc now, you know."

"Great. I'll wait here until you're ready, then let me buy you some supper."

"I have a better idea. Here's the key to my apartment. Take a cab to 306 Chelsea. Go to Apartment 6-B on the first floor. Relax, watch TV and I'll be home around four. Then we can go to eat." Her eyes were shining brightly. "It's so good to see you, Chad. Talking on the phone just doesn't work. Really, though, why did you come to Cambridge?"

"I'll see you at four. Then we can talk, okay?" He leaned on his cane, a stray lock of hair dangled on his forehead.

"You look great, sir. See you then." She watched him make his way to the front. He had gained a little weight, she noticed. His limp wasn't too bad. She'd check him out later.

Mary was back from her break and Mrs. Wollen was waiting to be called in to see the doctor. Amy went in a side door and buzzed Mary who led Mrs. Wollen into an examining room where she was weighed. Mary took her blood pressure, asked her some questions and jotted on a clipboard. Then Mary left her for Dr. Crowley.

Amy locked up, told Mary she'd see her on Monday and to have a nice weekend. She made her way to her car humming to herself.

Pleasant cooking aromas greeted her outside her apartment door which was partly open. Kicking off her shoes she headed to the kitchen in her stocking feet. Chad was stirring a pot of something that smelled like heaven.

Standing next to him she caught a faint smell of coconut body wash. "What's that?"

"It's coconut. You had lavender, but I thought the coconut was more, you know, me." He smiled down at her. His hair was damp and curly and uncombed.

"No, I meant in the pot."

"Oh. You said to relax which is all I've been doing for months. So I showered and decided to see if you had food. Bingo. I found a piece of steak which I diced, cut up some potatoes, carrots and onions, some bottles of herbs were over there, a beef bouillon cube and voila. We don't have to go out to eat. You even had enough lettuce and tomato for a small salad." He was proud of himself.

"Bless you, Bosley. I really would rather shower and stay here. Know what? I have a fresh rye bread from the bakery around the corner. I got it this morning because I ran out. I must have toast in the a.m." She poked him in the shoulder.

"Sounds good. I'll get the butter out to soften."

"Nice shirt." He was wearing a dark blue cotton and nylon casual shirt covered with bright yellow hibiscus. "That's very Hawaiian."

"It's for my interview. The Park Commission administrator who was supposed to see me in Washington called. Said he had an appointment in Boston this weekend. He wants me to go to the National Parks office tomorrow afternoon at three. Thought I'd wear the shirt to suggest Hawaii, maybe." He laughed.

"Well, it is cute. But, flowers? What do you think?"

"I have a back-up one. It's black with pineapples."

She giggled. "You're crazy, you know. Maybe you're not quite over your trauma. Were you always like this?"

"I also have a suit," he said seriously. "I'll put on a fashion show for you later." He winked.

She rolled her eyes as she made her way to the bedroom. "I have to take a shower."

Chad set the little table by the kitchen window. He made fresh coffee. Amy came back to the kitchen in a robe and a fluffy white towel wrapped around her wet hair.

"So, you'll stay with me tonight?" Her cheeks were bright pink from the hot shower.

"Thanks, I'd like that." He invaded her space. "God, you're beautiful, Doc." He gently removed the towel from her hair and put it around her shoulders. He ran his fingers through her damp curls. She untied her sash and let her robe fall around her ankles.

"Let me check your leg, Chad." She took his hand and led him toward the bedroom. He reached over and turned off the stew.

As he lay back against the pillows, Amy ran her fingers over his ankle, up his shin bone to his knee. Tapping her fingers professionally against the bones, she put her palm behind his calf and pulled his leg up. She frowned.

"No, Doc. No frowns and no mmms. Just you and me." He sounded worried. "You're right, the phone relationship doesn't cut it. I've missed you so much. You're all I think about."

She decided to delay her prognosis for just a little while longer. Lying beside him, she stretched her full length against his side, unbuttoned his hibiscus splashed shirt, and rubbed her hand across his wide chest and flat stomach. He moaned and rolled over on top of her.

Amy let him sleep while she padded into the kitchen and turned the stew back on low. She headed back to the shower.

The shower door opened and Chad stepped in. He put liquid soap on his hand and rubbed her body until it was covered with foam. She leaned her body against him, surrounded with steam, and she whispered, "You're so sweet, Chad."

"This will be longer, I promise." He thrust against her again and again, slowly deliberately, until finally exhausted Amy reached over and turned off the spray that was now just lukewarm.

"The stew is delicious." She dabbed a piece of bread into the juice. "You're hired. Imagine coming home to a meal like this after a hard day at the hospital."

"Now wait a minute. Just because I wore a shirt with flowers…don't forget, I'll be putting in long hours at the park, probably wrestling bears." He grinned widely.

"Therein lies a problem." She looked down at her plate. They both grew quiet.

"Yeah, I know. We may have to go with a long distance relationship for a while longer. I would hate it, though." He sighed.

"What time is your meeting again?"

"At three. Why don't you come with me. Afterwards we can go to a movie, have some dinner, whatever." He reached over and took her hand. "Just don't frown, okay?"

"Look, do me a favor. See if the administrator can delay your start time until after the first of the year. I'm sure you'll get the position, but…"

"But that's six months from now, Amy. Why would I do that? I really want this. It's something I've been ready for since I was a young man."

"You are a young man. Don't be in such a rush. I think your shin needs to be re-set. It just doesn't feel right to me. Tomorrow morning we'll go to X-ray and have some pictures taken, okay? Humor me." She got up and caressed his head against her breast. "It feels like it's been stressed. Let's be sure."

"Yes, doctor." He put his arms around her waist and nuzzled her chest. "I admit it hasn't felt good for the last few months."

"You should have said something." He looked so glum she took his hand and they went back to the bedroom. The stew got cold.

Amy got the technician to squeeze them in for a series of pictures. She asked the orthopedic surgeon to consult with Dr. Sam Carter at Duke. By noon, Amy knew that Chad's bone needed to be reset. The surgeon, after speaking with Sam, was convinced he should wait for Sam to send him a software program that he and Brian Harcher developed. It was a brand new approach for developing stronger stress points. Sam promised to send it by overnight mail.

"The good news," the doctor told Chad, "is that the healing time is cut in half.

"When can you do the procedure, doctor?" Chad sounded eager to get it done.

"Tuesday morning. Be here by six. Dr. Crowley, you'll handle the paper work?" She agreed.

"What is the hospital recovery time, Doctor?" Amy asked.

"Two days, maybe three. Then he can go home to continue to heal. We'll give him a short cast, then a boot. This new procedure reduces healing time because there is less invasive surgery. In three months, he'll be just fine. No stress on that leg, though. That's a must." He looked directly at Chad.

He followed her to the business office. "I have good insurance, Amy. My Dad always carried good coverage for all the men because of the nature of the work. I kept it up when I sold the company."

"That's great. Let's get the pesky paper work done then head to your interview so you can get everything settled with the Power Ranger."

"I hope he'll understand. But, he's waited this long for me, I guess a few months more shouldn't make too much difference." Chad sounded concerned.

"Please don't worry. I'm sure everything will work out for you." Amy was confident because she already spoke with the administrator by phone while Chad's doctor was explaining the details of his condition. She swore the director to confidentiality.

Chapter 61

Barry and Jenna Kretzler sat on their new sofa in their new home in a gated community in northern Westchester, New York. Jenna did most of her medical recording at home on her new computer. If she wanted her baby to go full term she had to stay at home, relax and take her medicine. Barry wanted her to quit her job but she insisted that it made her happy and her weekly visits to the medical records office were social as well as dropping off and picking up her assignments.

Jenna got up and went to the kitchen. "Want some pop-corn? I have the low fat kind."

Barry started to get up. "Let me get it. I can't stand it when you're always jumping up and doing things. You have so much nervous energy."

She pointed a finger at him and said, "Give me five minutes. I need to work off my antsiness."

He settled back with a mixed drink. The news was on their wide screen TV. Peter Jackson was reporting on the sentencing proceedings handed down today in the case of the state versus Jerry Machlich and Craig Appleby, both men receiving the death penalty. In New York that meant lethal injection. Barry smiled. He knew earlier that they would get the death penalty but it felt good to hear it with thousands of other viewers.

Jenna came in with two bowls of steaming pop-corn. "Want to watch a movie?"

He stared at her. She was so beautiful. "You're the best thing that happened to me, Jenna. It's like my mom gave me life, then she gave me you."

"You forget I got you drunk at your mother's wedding then I took advantage of you. I had my way with you, young man," she said in a deep, foreign voice.

"Whatever. Come here. I need to hold you, both of you." He put his arms around her and held her tightly.

The entertainment segment came on with a preview of the coming Golden Globe awards.

"Oh, let's watch this. I love to see who's up for awards." She popped the kernels while he kept his arm around her.

The announcer went through the major nominees then said, "Also nominated for best score for a documentary is newcomer Marie Maneros of Blue Dreams Studio for her music in *Morning's Children*. The theme song, *Out of the Mist* is climbing the charts and expected to be in the top five at Golden Globe time. Miss Maneros is collaborating on a full length motion picture score with Paul Andrews, Production Manager of Blue Dreams."

The camera zoomed in on the table where Blue Dreams personnel sat at the nominations banquet. Marie looked radiant in a dark green, shimmering, low-cut gown. Paul Andrews, handsome in a tuxedo had one arm draped over the back of her chair, their heads together, talking and laughing.

Barry smiled. "Well, well, it looks like Marie is finally coming out of her shell."

Jenna's eyes went wide. "You know her?" Barry explained his relationship with Marie Maneros. "You remember when her teacher boyfriend died on the airplane. I told you about her then."

"Right, right. Now I remember. She's gorgeous. And he is quite the catch. What a handsome man. Barry, you think there's any sparks there?" She ate popcorn and took in every detail.

"Oh, look. That's Steven Spielberg shaking Paul's hand. He's leaning over and saying something to Marie Maneros. Oh, my God, imagine chatting with Spielberg. And that Paul Andrews, he's so handsome. Don't they look great together?"

In the background music swelled around the glittering crowd. "I love that song. It's so touching it brings tears to my eyes. It's about autistic children, you know. That's what their documentary is about." She put the popcorn on the side table and hugged Barry. "I hope our baby will be fine. I hate to think of anything…."

"Hey, you're healthy and so am I. The doctor said there was nothing to worry about except your potential to miscarry. That has nothing to do with the health of the baby." He held her close. "Tell you what, after you have our baby, we'll take a trip to San Diego. Marie would love to meet you." He laughed at the screen. "Never thought that shy little girl would become a celebrity, but, she is brilliant so, why not?"

Chapter 62

Hal sat at the restaurant bar. It was crowded but Michele said she made reservations. She was fashionably late, he noticed. Taking Chuck's letter out of his pocket, he read it again. It was mostly about the coming football season, the practices, the physicals and the studies. Chuck was a senior. He received scholarship offers from Florida, Pennsylvania, Nebraska and so on. Hal felt good. Chuck would be fine. The twins were entering high school this fall, and they'd be fine, too. His parents were in good health, so why did he feel apprehensive, like the other shoe needed to fall? Everything is going smoothly and he was spending time worrying about something vague, something not there. What it was, he couldn't grasp, but it felt palpable, real, but not solid, just a thought, a flicker of anxiety. At night he woke up sweating. He knew people suffered from panic attacks, but why him, and why now?

She tapped him on the shoulder. He jumped sideways with a start.

"Hey, hey, take it easy big guy. It's only little old me. Were you day dreaming or what?" Michele was short, but she made a mighty impact in her tight-fitting spaghetti-strapped little black dress with black and silver pumps. Her hair brushed her shoulders and framed her face. Long rhinestone earrings swayed among soft strands of hair. The effect was stunning. Hiking onto the stool next to him and crossing her sleek legs, he noticed guys looking at her approvingly.

"Shall we get to our table?" He took her arm and steered her off the stool over to the reservation desk.

"Michele Banks, party of two," she told the maitre'd who led them to a white linen covered table in a corner. The Minerva Lounge was one of the finest in the Fall River, Mass. area.

Over salads, Michele looked over at Hal. "So you like my idea of a thank-you dinner?"

"It wasn't necessary, but I feel like I'm the one who lucked out here. Did you get it all squared away?"

"Hal, Mr. Renner offered me a job in his new operation in Houston. As soon as I get my advanced architectural engineering degree I'm on my way. Six months tops. What do you think?"

"I think you're going to love my neck of the woods. Texas is great and construction is booming."

"What about you? Think you'll stay here at Liberty Core?" She sipped her lemon water.

"For the first time in over five years I feel unsure. Lately, I've been feeling sort of, I don't know, uneasy. Like, I love what I'm doing, so that's not it. I want to have my own core sampling lab and consulting firm. It's what I do best, but..." he shrugged his shoulders.

"You're not getting tired of playing in the dirt, are you?" She laughed, a deep crisp giggle.

"I'm not an analyst but you know what I think? I think I've been focused too long on the same things. When I finish this apprenticeship at Liberty, I'll receive my third engineering license. I think I'll take a break and go on a cruise or something silly like that."

Michele forked a piece of tomato and slipped it into her mouth. "Want company? I've been thinking of taking a little rest when I finish, too. Let's fly to Europe and take in the cathedrals, bridges, universities, and museums."

"Doesn't that sound like another assignment?" He seemed more relaxed.

"No. It sounds like an enjoyable jaunt by two professionals with cameras. Why waste an expensive trip....we could always use the photos for inspiration."

He bent his head to her. She was all business after all. Tough, purposeful and driven. "Tell you what. I'd like that, but I'll make a deal with you. If we concentrate half our time on elegant period hotels, the trip will be my treat." He looked at her questioningly.

"You're on, my man. Some of those old hotels are architectural wonders."

She thought about her mom, how she would love a trip like this. God, she missed her so much. Before she died, she won a lottery and gave it all to Michele. Seven hundred thousand dollars. It would have been more but three people had the same winning number combination in the Ohio lottery. By then, Ella Banks, single mom with one child, had lost her husband to the Gulf War and knew she needed an operation on a brain tumor. She gladly signed her share of the winnings into a trust for Michele. Ella died on the operating table.

He was staring at her. "Now who's daydreaming? Earth to Michele."

"Oh, nothing. Just little thoughts that come and go. We're quite a pair of dreamers, aren't we?"

"Is that what it is? Dreaming? My thoughts scare me at times like, you know, something is going to happen, and it's not good. I have no reason to gather that kind of wool, but I do."

"For me," she said, "it's already happened. The death of my mom was probably the worst thing that will ever happen to me. I don't know the future, and maybe there is more heading my way, but I doubt it. It took me a long time to recover from her passing."

He turned to her, held her gaze then hugged her tenderly. She felt soft, warm and comforting, like if he ever needed a shoulder, he'd want it to be Michele's.

Chapter 63

Dr. Donna Worden smelled the beautiful gardenia plant. It was enormous filling one corner of the waiting room. The gold ribbon splayed across the dark green shiny leaves read, "Congratulations and Good Luck." The card was signed by Michael Ridley and Edward Karetsky. She smiled up at Sam.

"It's from the money police. The roses are from my dad and the giant fern is from Brian Harcher. All with cards of good wishes."

Sam looked around the new waiting room. "If we get any more plants, we won't have any room for patients." He grinned as he fingered the leaves of the shiny plants musing on the thoughtfulness of the people around them.

"Oh, that reminds me. We have our first two appointments. Both from the newspaper ad. A high school senior football player with a dislocated disc and an elderly woman with sciatica." Donna showed him the appointment book. He leaned over the counter and ran his finger over the two appointments.

"This is so neat. I can handle the woman. I see she's here tomorrow morning. Then I need to be at Duke at two. I need to be there again at ten the next morning. So you can take the boy. Is that all right?" At this moment, Sam was happy that Donna was by his side working along with him to achieve the same goals.

The phone rang. Donna picked it up. "Spring Hill Orthopedics." She listened. Sam was pleased with the name. Their office was located in the Spring Hill section of the Tri-cities, Raleigh, Durham and Chapel Hill. "Yes, of course. I can give you an appointment next Tuesday, Mr. Baxter. Is 9 a.m. good for you? Fine. We'll see you then. Please bring a list of any medications you're taking. Bye."

She looked up. "Neck pain. We're on our way, Sam. Do you think we should hire a professional receptionist? One who can handle the insurance work. Maybe part time for now. She could field these calls and make appointments around our schedules."

"Do it. Let's get an ad together and I can drop it off tomorrow morning." He leaned down and hugged Donna. "You're right, girl. We are on our way."

Chapter 64

The thick book titled simply *Endocrinology* was open to the chapter on pituitary glands. Amy's eyes were tired. She knew she should be at the table sitting on a hard chair rather than trying to support the heavy book on her lap with her back deep in the overstuffed recliner.

"Are you awake?" she whispered to Chad who was stretched on the sofa, his head on two pillows, leg supported by a third. The short cast was snow white except for the notes in magic marker written by Sue and Martha when they visited after Chad's operation.

He stirred. "Hmmm. Just dozing a bit. You almost through studying?"

"Almost through." She closed the book and leaned her arm on it. "I've been thinking more than reading, though." She put the book on the end table and came over to him. He shifted and she sat on the edge of the sofa taking in his rugged good looks, his comforting presence and her reluctance to let him go when he was healed.

"You'll be getting your boot tomorrow." She ran her hand along the cast. "You'll be mobile again. I know you'll get the job with the Park Commission. Wherever you go, I'd like to tag along. I can be a doctor anywhere I hang out a shingle. I can study on the rocky coasts or next to a geyser. I will be an endocrinologist eventually, but right now I'd like to stay with you." Chad frowned. "Hear me out. There are hospitals everywhere just panting for good doctors and I'm a good doctor. An internship in endocrinology will be a breeze for me. I don't want to brag, but the worst is over for me. I've put in the long and arduous hours, the rotation shifts, and all the rest of it. The only field left, the one I really want, will be mine in due time."

He rose up on his elbow, "Doctor, you sure have a great bedside manner." She leaned over and kissed him. "But are you absolutely sure? I don't want to be a pain in the neck with the traveling around from park to park."

"It's a deal, then? You don't mind hanging around with a doctor who will have her nose in a book while eagles soar overhead?"

"What a picture. I can't wait for our first assignment. Are you sure you're ready for this? If it doesn't work out I will understand if you just pack up and leave the great outdoors for hospital halls."

She took his hand, "After seven years of concentrated study, two doctorates, all focus, I'm more than ready. Anyway, you need me near. What if a tree falls on you?"

Chapter 65

Chuck Jensen sat in the back yard of his home and talked quietly to his father. Charles smoked thoughtfully. He looked at his son proudly.

"So you think you'll be in the first ten draft pick? What have you heard?"

Chuck toyed with a can of coke. "I'll have to finish this school year. Scouts from the Eagles and the Packers have talked to me so far. Coach says I should wait a few weeks to see who else is interested. You know I want to play for the Rams, but I'll go where the money is, right?"

Charles laughed. "When you're looking at that kind of money, it shouldn't matter. If the Rams make a half-decent, competitive offer, go with it. Just promise me you'll get your degree, okay?"

"Sure, Dad. That's going to be part of the contract no matter who I sign with. I think I'll talk with Coach. He'll tell the Rams' scout I'm interested. Thanks, Dad. When are you and Mom going to Panama City?"

"Next week. We'll be there during the picks, but your Uncle Jamie has a wide screen TV so we won't miss a thing. We'll celebrate when we get back. We'll have a party."

Chuck swigged the soda. "So what's this plane charter costing you?"

"With eight people going it's not very much. Since we're going one-way it's only two hundred each. Uncle Jamie and Aunt Catherine will drive us back and spend a few weeks with us here. It should be fun. We'll fish and play golf and the ladies will lounge on the beach." Charlie crushed his cigarette and got up to go into the house. "We're proud of you, son. Your scholarship and now going pro, it's a father's dream. And most of all, it didn't cost us anything." He laughed and slapped Chuck on the shoulder.

Chuck faked a punch and said, "You got off real cheap between Hal and me, didn't you? You're one lucky son-of-a-gun and look at you. Spending two hundred dollars each, each, mind you, to go and sun in Panama City. There was a day when this conversation would never take place. I am glad to see that you and mom know how to have some fun once in a while. And as for that party, I might just be bringing a friend of mine I'd like you to meet."

Charlie laughed heartily and began a sing-song chant. "Chuckie's got a girlfriend."

He blushed. "Just Marlene from my Spanish class. She's a study partner but she turned into, as I said, a friend. You'll like her."

Chapter 66

Hal was working on some core samples in the lab of Liberty Core with his assistant, Larry, when the phone rang. Larry picked it up, spoke softly for a few moments then brought the phone over to Hal.

"It's for you, Hal." Larry was pale.

Hal squinted at Larry and mouthed 'Who?' at him. Larry put his eyes down turned, and left the room.

"This is Hal." His feelings of anxiety returned in a rush and washed over him.

"Hal, Hal, we don't know what to do. Come home, please, now." It was his sister Terry, sobbing hysterically.

"Terry, calm down. What is it? Tell me. You have to talk to me. Calm down, please." But he was frightened, too. He was imagining the worse possible scenarios, none of them good. He was trembling.

"It's Mom and Dad. They're dead, Hal, both of them, both of them." She was sobbing out the words, the fear and anguish taking over.

"What happened, Honey?" God, he wished he were in Brownsville right now instead of struggling with a stupid phone and feeling all this dread and confusion. On the other end it sounded as if the phone dropped.

"Hello," he shouted.

Tammy came on. She was a little more controlled but sounded weary from weeping. Her voice was husky and raspy.

"Their plane crashed in a wooded area near Pensacola. The…the…plane…it burst into flames, exploded. They're all dead, all nine people. How could this happen to us when everything was going so good?"

"You mean…" He couldn't finish. He just couldn't. "I'm coming home. Sometime today. You're at the Lorisons, right? I'll pick you up there." He hung up the phone and began to sob. He picked up one of the core samples and began to bang it on the lab counter.

Larry didn't know what to do. He came over and stood by Hal.

"Man, I'm really sorry. I can't even imagine the pain…"

Hal reached out to Larry who hugged him and let Hal cry on his shoulder, huge wracking sobs that shook through his body.

"It's okay. Let it out." Larry held him a few moments longer then gently pushed him away. "You know, I can't say the right stuff to you. It's going to be a rough few weeks ahead for you. But, once you told me you were the oldest. I guess that means you have to be the strongest. Those girls sound like they need a firm presence right now. And what about your brother, the football player? Why didn't he call you? You need to go to them. I'll talk to the boss. He'll understand. Let's close the lab, I'll take you to your place and then the airport. Leave your car here."

Hal was like a robot. He obeyed Larry who took over. On the way to the airport they stopped at MIT. Hal went to his counselor who said he'd take care of any extensions Hal needed. Then Hal called Michele. Somehow, telling her calmed him.

"How long will you be gone and is there anything you want me to do?" she asked.

"I don't know. Two to three weeks. There's so much to think about. I can't think straight. Everything keeps jumbling up on me. This is so hard, Michele, so hard." His voice broke.

"You need to be strong, Hal. Even if you don't feel it, you have to show it. You have to." She was emphatic. Like she knew from experience.

He sighed. "I guess life can't always be good. But this is too much. We were all so happy, so content. Why doesn't it ever last, Michele?"

Chapter 67

Chuck sat next to Hal, the two girls beside him. The memorial service for Charles and Jean Jensen was inspiring, comforting and beautiful. Marie Maneros Andrews was there. She played a cantata on the organ that was magnificent. Edward Karetsky sat in a pew in the back along with Michael Ridley.

"If there is anything we can do," they said. Hal asked them to handle all the finances. They agreed.

Hal looked around St. Patrick's Church. It was overflowing with flowers from the various clubs and organizations with which his parents had been affiliated. The neighborhood was there as well as friends of Hal, Chuck and the girls. The seats were filled. Somehow, being in the church, surrounded by old friends, relatives, even strangers, made Hal feel calm inside.

He stared at the photos of his parents near the altar. What were the reasons they were gone entered his mind. Does there have to be a reason? They were such a nice looking couple. All these thoughts going through his mind. It just happened. Now...he looked at his parents and wondered what they would want him to do. I need time, but I'll sort it out, whatever it is. His eyes welled up and the photo became a kaleidoscope of candlelight and flowers.

The music rose to a finale, the priest had a parting prayer and it was over. Traditionally, the family went to the casket for a last goodbye, then walked down the aisle to wait outside for the rest of the mourners to come out, then thanked everyone for attending. Since there were no caskets, the congregation sat and waited for the Jensens to leave the church first.

Outside, the four children of Charles and Jean Jensen began the ritual of hugs, handshaking and kissing. They accepted all the condolences graciously.

Then she was standing in front of him, hand outstretched, silent. It was more than Hal could bear. "Michele? You came. I don't know what to say."

She hugged him as he cried softly into her shoulder. "Don't say anything. I'll see you later at your house." She left. He saw her get into a rental car and leave the parking lot. Hal continued talking to well-wishers.

The girls were in their rooms upstairs, Chuck was in the back yard with friends, and Hal was in the kitchen with his Uncle Jamie and Aunt Catherine.

"Don't make any plans yet, son," his uncle was saying. They all had plates of food left by the neighbors.

His Aunt Catherine's eyes were red-rimmed. "You're all welcome to come stay with us for as long as you like. Our home is yours."

"And we appreciate that Aunt Catherine. But the girls have to finish school here. I wouldn't want to uproot them now. All their friends are here, they're doing well in school. They'll be juniors this September, so they only have two more years to go. They should graduate from Brownsville like we all did."

Hal wandered out back. Chuck was at the picnic table. A few of his friends were getting ready to leave. Two sat at the table with Chuck.

"We're going to miss your folks. They were always there, you know," a tall gangly, awkward boy said.

The other one looked at Hal. "Mr. Jensen always had those hard candies on him. Sometimes, when I wasn't looking, he'd throw one at me."

Hal laughed. He remembered the hard candies. He got hit by more than one. The two boys shook hands with Chuck and Hal and they drifted toward the house.

"You okay, Chuck?" Hal slid onto the bench seat across from his brother.

"No, I'm sure not okay. I never will be again. What is it all about, Hal? Why do you think this had to happen? What's the use?" He began to sob softly.

"We have to go on. Mom and Dad would want us to finish what we started, what they started, really. All their hopes for us have to come true. It's the only way we have of honoring their memory. They had the chance to see us heading in the right direction. We can't stop now. You need to play ball, I need to get my own firm, and the girls need to graduate and go on."

"I think you're right. Dad and I sat at this table before they went on vacation. He was really thrilled about my wanting to play for the Rams. Coach Adams said to hold out for it. They'll make deals until they can draft me. My first touchdown will be for Dad." His eyes were wet.

Terry called from the back porch, "Hal, there's a Michele Banks here to see you."

Hal got up, put a hand on Chuck's shoulder and said, "Things might be changing in this family, but from here on, it's going to be for the good. I promise."

Hal left with Michele in her rental car. They drove around Brownsville.

"What made you show up here? Not that I mind at all. I'm glad you came because somehow, I find comfort in your presence. But I must admit, I was surprised that you came all the way to Brownsville."

"It's where I felt I had to be. I've been thinking, mostly crazy thoughts, but here goes. In September I'll be starting work at Renner's Corporate Headquarters south of Houston. That's about forty-five minutes from here. Chuck will be away at football camp by then. Let me move in with you. I need a place anyway and I can help with the girls."

He looked at her for a long moment. "You know, drive me over to the airport. Continue down this street then make a right at the ramp."

She did. They were on the interstate. "Now, pretty soon we'll see a sign for the airport ramp. Take it."

They stood at the observation window and looked out at the planes landing and taking off.

"Last time I was home my Dad was talking about some political scuttlebutt involving a project for a few landing strips to expand the airport. The town was looking for a grant." Hal's voice became excited. "Look at the room they have out there. I have to find out what happened."

"What are you thinking? Having Liberty put in a bid to do the core work? Hal, that's brilliant. An airport. You're looking at seven years of work, at least. Who can you ask?"

"Our neighbor, Buzz Taylor is on the city planning board. I'll call him tomorrow, then I'll call Hank at Liberty," Hal said. He took Michele's hand. "With the two of us at the house, the girls will graduate and we can guide them into fields that suit their capabilities. Your timing is impeccable, you know."

Buzz Taylor offered his condolences again. He and his wife had been at the Memorial service. "We have been offered a grant and we're in the process of buying up those two farms. There's a possibility of getting more land on the north side of the terminal. If we do, we'll be constructing a new terminal, too. What can I help you with, Hal?"

"I was wondering about the bidding process. The firm I'm with is Liberty Core. We do environmental studies, EPA regs, core samples, deep drilling…."

"Hal, no one has even talked about those areas yet. I suspect you'll be first in. Does Liberty have anything in the southwest?"

"We're planning a consulting firm here in Brownsville. I'll get back to you, okay?" The two men shook hands and Hal walked next door.

Michele was having salad at the table with the girls. He said, "Get on the phone and call Renner. Ask him if you could draft plans for a terminal to submit to bid next month. You'll be right here in Houston to oversee the process."

"Give me the phone. I'll call Renner right now."

Tammy and Terry went to the church with three of their friends.

Father Mark asked them to attend grief counseling sessions held every Wednesday. Tammy and Terry needed more support than Hal was prepared to give them. It would be a long, complicated summer, he knew. How could he rebuild the girls' confidence?

Chapter 68

The black Lincoln town car pulled into the Jensen's driveway. Hal and Michele were on the wide front porch, Jean Jensen decorating touches all around them. The wicker porch swing, freshly painted just a month ago, geraniums in white pots, three white rocking chairs and a coat of marine grey on the floor that Charlie finished a mere two weeks ago gave the porch a look of class. Hal put his drink on the little wrought iron table and went to the edge of the porch expectantly.

"Well, look at you Marie," Hal called out.

She got out of the car and ran to Hal. They hugged and hugged. Hal welled up. Marie rubbed his shoulders. She was such a comfort. She really was her music. Ease and solace seemed to surround her tiny frame.

"Hal, there's someone I want you to meet." Paul hung back a little. Now he stepped forward with his hand outstretched. "This is my husband, Paul Andrews."

"I guess everyone has heard of you, Paul. A pleasure to meet you. And congratulations, you two." Hal shook Paul's hand warmly. My brother and two sisters are making some lunch. Join us."

They walked up to the porch. Hal said, "I'd like you to meet a colleague of mine, Michele Banks. This is Marie Maneros Andrews and her husband, Paul."

Michele was delighted. "I watch all the awards shows. I see you at your table all the time. You've won quite a few trophies, too. I love all your music. That documentary you did, *Morning's Children* was so inspiring. And the theme song, *Out of the Mist* blows me away every time I hear it. You must lead an exciting life."

"It is exciting," Marie said. "But, it's hard work and late hours, too. Sometimes a real grind when we have a deadline."

Chuck poked his head out the door, "Lunch is on the table in the back yard."

"Chuck, come here a minute. I'd like you to meet Paul and Marie Andrews. Marie was also a recipient of the Romans-Burkas scholarship."

Chuck shook hands. "Marie Maneros. I love your music. It's brand new, lots of feeling. I have the tape with *Wrapped in Time* on it. It's my favorite."

"Thanks, Chuck. I'll send you a copy of my, I should say, our latest album. Paul and I collaborated on it for an upcoming Ron Howard movie about the Alaskan coasts.

Paul put his hand on Chuck's back. "And I have been watching your progress, Chuck. Where do you think you'll be reporting to training camp?"

"If all goes well, the Rams should pick me up. It's where I want to play and it was my father's favorite team."

They sat at the picnic table and ate Terry and Tammy's home made chili and ham sandwiches. The girls were overwhelmed by Marie and Paul. They were full of questions. Hal was grateful to see some of their old animated selves again.

Hal leaned over to Marie. "Where are you two staying tonight because I want you to stay here. A sleepover will do the girls a world of good."

"Then we'll do it." She looked over at Paul who nodded his assent. "But we do have to get back tomorrow. Tons of work, you know. Do you have room?"

She pushed a strand of hair behind her ear. Hal thought she looked so beautiful. Her skin was radiant. What a long way she has come since that first day in Ridley's office.

"This is a five bedroom house. Remember, my folks had four kids. There are two bathrooms on the second floor and one on the first. The girls can bunk together. Chuck and I will use his bedroom, Michele can use Tammy's room and you and Paul can have the master bedroom. That still leaves another bedroom free in case we need it." Hal was insistent.

"And the sofa opens to a bed." Marie laughed. "My grandma always said that when we had company."

Terry asked Marie softly, "That song, *Out of the Mist*, how did you think of that? It's so gorgeous. I could see how it won awards."

"It's because of the children who couldn't speak, isn't it? They are like in a fog or something." Tammy blushed at her little attempt at understanding.

"That is part of it, Tam, but there's more. All of us are, in one way or another living in a mist until something comes along and clears our eyes. Then we find our voice and express ourselves in all kinds of ways. I often think that people's lives are like different types of music. Some live a concert, a symphony, a comic opera, or, like in the case of the five of us scholarship recipients, a rhapsody, so sweet it hurts. We make a career choice, a love, or a strong drive to accomplish something. Even in silence, there is expression, like the autistic children. Each time one of them accomplishes even a little, it's an achievement of worth. What the song expresses, is the desire to find one's voice, and use it to make a mark that might be remembered even after we're gone."

"Yoo-hoo!" A shout from the side of the house. Everyone grew quiet and watched the corner. "They're all back here. I told you."

Hal got up to greet the young lady when Barry Kretzler came around the side of the house. "Hal, Hal. I don't know what to say, buddy." He hugged Hal. "I'm so sorry for your dreadful loss."

"I know, Barry. I appreciate your coming here. How did you know?"

"Larry, your lab assistant. My name and number was on your desk, so he called me. I'm glad that he did."

Hal introduced Barry and Jenna Kretzler. More plates were set. The conversation was active, Jenna couldn't get enough of Marie. She and

Tammy and Terry cornered Marie with dozens of questions. Michele felt somehow left out until Jenna asked her if she worked with Hal.

"Not in the same capacity. He protects work sites, I design them. It's a joint effort, and we both play in the dirt, but I create." She seemed uncertain until Jenna and Marie shifted interests.

"Paul and I want to live in a home we build together in southern California, but we're not sure what we want. Maybe you could help us."

"Just tell me your idea of a dream house and I'll send you some plans. We'll talk about your life style and I'll include some interior floor plans." Michele was on her own turf now and her voice reflected it.

"Let's do it, Paul." She sounded eager.

"Sure," he agreed. "We can grab some together time tonight and list what we think we want."

Hal smiled. "And I'll make sure it doesn't slide down the side of a hill or end up in the Pacific." Everyone laughed.

Barry interjected, "Jenna and I are looking to build in upstate New York. We'd like a country home something like this one."

"You have strong ground in that part of the country. Get a core sample anyway, and EPA approval."

"I can send you some plans, too. No problem," she said as she took a second bowl of chili.

Tammy was thoughtful. "How can you design all these houses so fast, Michele?"

"I use computer programs I get from an outfit in California. The programmer is brilliant. I can do the whole thing in minutes by arranging it all on spread sheets first."

"Is it Harcher, by any chance?" Hal giggled.

"Yes it is. How did you know? Do you use Harcher?"

Barry nodded his head. "I keep track of crime with Harcher."

"I couldn't transcribe music without him," Marie said warmly. "Bless Brian Harcher. Do any of you get to Bluff View?"

"Jenna and I spent our honeymoon there. It's still a great place to vacation. The Karetskys and the Ridleys are wonderful hosts." Barry sipped his lemonade.

"Unfortunately, I have been way too busy. I know Sam goes once in a while during the summers. Amy has been there to fish with her dad. I keep promising myself to go for a few days. Maybe before September. Right now, Michele and I have a few irons in the fire." Hal told them about the projects at the airport.

Tammy sat next to Michele on the couch and talked to her about design. Tammy was fascinated. "What should I study in high school? What courses should I take? You know, so I could do what you do."

Michele was flattered. "Math, of course. Drafting and blueprinting if your school offers it. And don't forget computer skills. That's getting to be the heart of designing. I can help you..." Michele stopped. The girls didn't know of the plan for Michele to move in come September.

Terry was quiet. Now she curled up on the arm chair across from Michele. "After the house is designed, and the floor plans are in place, what next?"

"Well, if your client wants to go one more step, they hire an interior decorator. Someone who is good at using the existing space, furniture arrangement, color, texture, lighting, and art work. It's the finishing touch that pulls the entire project together."

"Terry, you'd be good at that." Tammy giggled. "She dresses like a gypsy," she said to Michele.

Terry's eyes went wide. "I do. I love to mix colors. And if I wear a bulky sweater, I always top it with a filmy scarf."

"That's because you're a freakazoid," Tammy shook her head knowingly.

"Girls, be nice." Michele held up a hand. "Terry, take blueprinting, computers and art. When you apply to design school next year, you'll be way ahead of the game."

Hal looked away from Marie, Paul and Jenna. The girls were actually giggling with Michele. He smiled as he made his way over.

"Ladies, Chuck is already in bed. It's after eleven. The grown-ups need to talk some business." Hal pointed to the staircase.

"But we want to know how it all happens. Please, let us just stay an hour. We promise not to say one single word." Tammy was impassioned. Terry just held her breath.

"I have no objection," Michele shrugged.

"Nor do I," said Paul. 'It might do them some good to watch the process." Marie agreed, also.

"No giggling. I dislike giggling. Absolutely no giggling." Barry pointed at the two girls and frowned.

They near choked trying not to giggle. "Okay. We promise, Mr. Kretzler." Terry was blushing.

"Uncle Barry to you, young lady. And don't you forget it." he did a great impression of Groucho Marx.

They lasted until midnight. The girls were exhilarated but exhausted. At one a.m. the Jensen home was dark. Hal lay awake, though. He felt better, but couldn't sleep. He knew the girls would like having Michele around. He was planning to turn one bedroom into a drafting room. The three of them could use it. Chuck sighed audibly in his sleep.

Chapter 69

It was early, just eight thirty when Michael Ridley and Edward Karetsky drove quietly into the crowded Jensen driveway. They parked behind a new Lincoln town car.

"Let's not wake them, Edward. Yesterday was a long day for them." Michael carried a briefcase and a coffee in a plastic covered cup.

"Nice porch. We can wait here. It's very pleasant." Edward set down his cup and white paper bag on the wrought iron table. They sat on rocking chairs munching on Danish and sipping hot coffees.

"What do you think, Michael. Are we walking into an emotional powder keg?" Edward gazed across the front yard to the quiet street.

"Hal's always been rock solid. I guess the rest of them are, too. The parents were careful people. They made sure the kids were taken care of. Our kind of people, Edward." Michael brushed white crumbs from his navy suit jacket.

Both men had steely white hair, neatly combed. Their watches flashed at their wrists.

"I hear voices inside. It's after nine. Guess I should ring the bell." Edward rose. He put his finger on the doorbell just as the door opened. Michele stood in the doorway.

"Can I help you? I'm Michele Banks, a house guest of Hal." She had her hair in a pony tail.

"We're here to see Hal. I'm Michael Ridley and this is my partner, Edward Karetsky, from Chicago."

In the background Hal called out, "Michael, Edward, come on in. We're just making breakfast. Join us. Just about the whole crew is here."

"We would love to and we will, but first, can Edward and I speak to you, Chuck, Tammy and Terry privately? I'm sorry, Miss Banks, but it's a financial matter." Michael blushed.

"It's okay. Someone needs to start breakfast anyway. We have guests who will be leaving this morning." She headed for the kitchen.

Hal led the men into the den. "I'll go up and get Chuck and the girls."

Tammy's long blonde hair was disheveled. Terry had hers in a pony tail. They had robes over their pajamas. Both were barefoot. Chuck hulked in wearing shorts and a faded blue shirt. He was barefoot, too.

Edward began. "We are both terribly sorry for your loss. It's an extremely difficult time, we realize, but Hal did ask us to take care of all the financial aspects."

Michael opened his briefcase on the end table. He pulled out a folded blue document, opened it and said, "These are insurance papers and, these are your parents' wills. They are simple documents. We will leave them with you."

The girls huddled next to each other. Chuck's shoulders sagged, he looked wretched. He raised his head and caught Hal's eye. Hal looked grim, but strong. Chuck rallied.

"Sorry guys," Hal said. "These legal things, they just bring it all back so strongly. Like, it's real all over again."

"It's not the easiest part of our job. But it's necessary. Essentially," Michael went on holding the papers open, "and I'll get to the core of all this quickly. Hal, as the oldest will become owner of the house and everything in it, or attached to it. If the property is sold, the profits are to be shared equally. Hal is beneficiary of the insurance policies which, together, total two hundred and fifty thousand dollars. Basically, that's it. Your parents are to be respected for their vision. You are well-provided for. Hal, do you understand?"

"I do, Michael. Chuck, I plan to live here at least until the girls are on their own. The house will be ours until we four decide when it's time to sell it. As for the money, I don't need it, neither do you. You will be playing pro football this fall. I propose we put the money in trust for Tammy and Terry until they're twenty one."

"I agree, Hal. I won't need the money. Let's do what you said. How do we go about it?"

Hal looked at Edward and Michael. "Any ideas, boys?"

Michael smiled. "Of course. We'll take care of all the paper work, then we'll send them to you to sign."

"See how easy, Chuck. Remember these fellows when you're rolling in all that football dough."

Edward handed Chuck a Ridley and Ridley Associates card and said, "Anytime we can be of service to you we will be happy to hear from you."

"I never even thought about it. I guess I'm going to have to though, right?" Chuck blinked as he stared at the card.

"We would be honored to have you as a client. A few of the Chicago Bears use our firm." Michael coughed. "Of course, Hal, you know that the insurance money and Chuck's money are subject…."

"To the four percent fee. I know. Chuck, trust me. Whatever they take they earn back for you, plus. That's a guarantee." Hal laughed.

Tammy spoke up, "So how do we pay for our education if we have to wait until we're twenty one?"

Terry agreed. "We're only going to be seventeen and a half when we graduate. We'll be finished with school before we're twenty one."

Edward nodded at the girls. "Hal can have us word it so money can be taken out of the trust for any use approved by him. Would that work?"

Hal smiled along with Michael and Edward. "These girls don't miss a trick, do they?"

Terry said, "Could we get some kind of an allowance while we go to school? What did you call it? A stipend?"

Hal patted her on the shoulder and agreed. "Yes, with some control, though."

Chapter 70

Amy leaned against one of the boulders that lined the Maine coast. The waves crested and broke down the slope from where she sat. In the distance the deep red sun was beginning to rise above the horizon casting a red and orange ray across the sparkling ocean. She held her medical journal open on her lap and turned to gaze at Chad. His eyes were bright with the morning glow, his skin tan and weathered.

"Imagine being assigned to Acadia first. Isn't it wonderful?"

He took her hand. They were awash in shades of red, orange and yellow. "I'm so glad you're with me. I know it's selfish of me, but now that you're in my life I can't envision traveling around the country without you and enjoying it as much as I do. You're my center, my whole life."

"It's not selfish, Chad. I was ready for a change and this one is spectacular. Look at those waves and that sunrise putting on a show for us."

They watched the gulls and raptors diving for their first meals of the day. Chad leaned over and kissed her. "Do you realize that sitting on this outcropping might make us the first couple in America to greet the sun?"

"What a nice thought. I'm marrying a poet and he don't know it." She put her book on a ledge and wrapped her arms around his shoulders. "Want to put on a show for the gulls?"

"What time will your dad be getting to Bar Harbor?" he asked as he ran his hand along her thigh.

"Oops. In about two hours. I have to meet them at the Cliffside. Ceil knows how to get there. She's been here once before. Are you nervous?"

"A little. But if he likes to fish I have it made. I'll take him to Crystal Cove. We should have a dream fishing trip."

"I think I covered all the bases. We have the rooms, the flowers, the judge and the dinner all taken care of." Amy's eyes shone. "Just get back in time to dress, okay? I don't want to marry Smokey the Bear. Not good for the photos." She flicked the brim of his wide ranger hat.

He winked at her. "We'll get back in plenty of time. Not to worry."

Chapter 71

Ceil and Amy fussed with setting up the little room at the Cliffside Inn that Chad and she rented for their wedding. There were flowers in every corner, candles on the table with white linen and crystal goblets. She thought it all looked beautiful.

"Now, I need to get showered and dressed. Help me, Ceil?"

"Of course. I'll get your dress ready, you go ahead and shower. I'm just about ready. I'll slip into my beige suit and pin on the corsage your father bought me at the airport."

Amy looked at Ceil. "You and Dad are happy, right? Everything is good between you?"

"He still gets depressed, but less and less as time goes on. I try to keep us moving around. The local AARP has trips and we try to go on as many as possible. We always had a lot of fun when there were four of us, now we try to keep that spirit alive." Ceil sighed.

"Thank you, Ceil. For being there, for caring for us. We're both lucky to have you in our lives."

"Stop it, Amy. If this mascara runs I'll look like a train wreck," Ceil said as she put a tissue under her eyes.

She smoothed the dress on the hanger. It was a soft white chiffon with a sateen underlay, uneven hem, a v-neckline outlined in tiny seed pearls and sequins. Ceil answered a tap at the door. It was the young man who would provide the keyboard music.

"My name is Al. I just wanted to know beside the traditional Brahms, is there another selection the bride might like?"

Ceil thought a moment. It had been Ellie's favorite song. "Do you have the music for *Ave Maria*?"

"Oh, sure. That's a popular one. I'll be happy to play it. See you in a half hour."

Amy's hair was up, curly, little strands loose and flowing. Tiny white flowers outlined her top curls. She looked breathtaking. She and Ceil approached the private room with the gorgeous view of the setting sun. Everything looked fabulous, except Chad and Ted were missing.

"I'm so sorry, Judge Thomas. They were supposed to be here in time, but..." she stopped and followed the Judge's gaze to the doorway. Chad hurried to her side. Ted sheepishly went to Ceil with an I'm sorry scrunch on his face.

Amy took her father's arm and said, "Come lead me into the room, Dad. And you, Smokey the Bear, wait here by Judge Thomas."

Ted led Amy into the room to the strains of Brahms. He shook Chad's hand and Amy kissed her father before he went back to Ceil's side.

Soft strains of *Ave Maria* played in the background of the simple ceremony. They exchanged vows and rings. Chad kissed the bride. They walked to the vast window overlooking the crashing breakers of the Atlantic.

Amy looked up at Chad, into his glorious eyes. "I'll love you forever, Chad. You make life interesting. I have a hunch it's going to be quite a journey."

He took her hand and fingered the ring, "I owe you my life. I don't want to be an obstacle to you, ever. I realize you have ambitions, and I may not be able to keep up. But I promise never to be in your way."

"You'll keep up. And I promise, if I get too driven, it will never be at your expense. Let's love this way forever." She leaned against his arm.

Ceil wiped her eyes. She looked at Ted and squinted, "So, what happened? Fishing too good to leave?"

Ted smiled at her. "No, that wasn't it. Chad and I had a good old-fashioned man to man talk. We just lost sight of the time."

Ceil giggled, "That ranger friend of Chad's had the best time taking the pictures. I'm sure Chad will never live down getting married in his ranger uniform.

Over dinner, Ceil asked, "Is there going to be a honeymoon?"

"Sort of," said Amy. "I have to go to Chicago for a meeting of the Romans-Burkas Foundation Board. We'll get our business done there and then go on to Glacier National Park. That's going to be Chad's assignment next year."

Ted looked at Amy. "What about your endocrinology studies?" He sounded a little anxious.

"Before we leave here I'll have my certification from Bangor Memorial Hospital. I haven't been fishing all this time, Dad." Amy laughed.

"She's a whiz, Ted. She never ceases to amaze me, taking out the boat to fish, studying those big, impossible books and treating campers' injuries at the Ranger station. I found Wonder Woman, you know." Chad put his hand over Amy's.

Over dessert Amy coughed softly. Ceil, I don't know how to say this without sounding ungrateful, but we want you and Dad to have our wedding presents."

"Amy, Why?" Ceil was dumbfounded.

"Well, Chad and I are going to be living in and around national parks, in cabins, even lighthouses. And listen to what we received. The Kretzlers sent us a gorgeous silver tea service.

Ceil's eyes went wide. "Oh, my." Ted just chuckled.

"And," Amy went on, "Sam Carter, bless his heart, had his mom embroider a sixty by a hundred and twenty inch linen tablecloth." Chad rolled his eyes.

"The Andrews went all out and shipped us a fifty-six set of cut crystal stemware, the most beautiful thing I've ever seen." By now everyone was laughing out loud.

"Anything else?" Ted choked with giggles.

Amy couldn't finish. She was convulsed with laughter.

Chad continued, "From the Karetskys we got a complete set of stainless steel cookware and the Ridleys came through with shitake dinnerware."

Amy almost fell out of her chair. "Noritake, dear. Shitake are mushrooms." She took a drink of wine, then lifted her glass. "To Dad and Ceil who wisely provided us with two Hudson Bay blankets, thank you very much, and the Wilsons who sent a kit of outdoor knives, compasses, first aid kit, a subscription to National Geographic and a year's supply of trail mix."

"Here, here," Chad lifted his glass.

As they toasted and chatted, Amy, who faced the arched doorway into their reception room, became aware of a cluster of people talking to a waiter. They carried wrapped gifts. Behind three strange men with freshly combed hair, very wet, clean-shaven but with nicks here and there, she recognized Martha, Susan and Mark Wilson.

One of the men, a short one, was getting a bit loud. Amy looked across the table and scrunched her face at Chad. "You are in for a pleasant surprise. Get up and turn around slowly. Prepare for an onslaught."

They both got up and headed for the door. Chad was completely surprised. He never expected his Aunt Sue and cousins to make the trip. They told him they'd let him know and that was the last he heard.

"Our mare foaled early, so here we are, pal." Mark shook Chad's hand.

Rusty, Jim the foreman, and Frank from limbing never responded to his invitation.

"You invited us and here we are. We represent your old crew. Only ones with enough time saved up to take this little vacation." Rusty looked around and Chad half expected him to spit a string of tobacco juice.

"I really am happy you boys could make it. Come on in and sit down."

Amy quietly dodged out of the room and went to the office in front where she ordered six meals and three rooms for their new guests.

When she returned, everyone had been introduced, the waiters were wheeling in desserts and coffees.

"Boys, you need to meet Dr. Amy Crowley, the lady that saved my life and my sanity when I had the wreck. The new Mrs. Chad Fergis." He beamed at Amy proudly.

"We all heard what you did. Mrs. Wilson called from time to time and kept us updated. You did right by Chad, Dr. Crowley. We all hope you two will be very happy. He's a great guy and was a fair, fine boss." Rusty was red, the other men nodded in agreement.

"Your food will be here momentarily. Meantime, you need to toast us," Amy said as she poured some wine into their glasses.

"Open your gift, boss. The boys all chipped in and got you something they thought you could use. By the way, did you wear that outfit for the wedding?" Rusty looked Chad up and down.

"It's a long story, guys. If you have some time tomorrow morning, maybe you could do some fishing with Ted here. He knows a great spot where you'd get a lot of action and lose track of the time." Chad looked over at Ted with raised eyebrows.

"Sure. Ceil and I don't leave until late afternoon. I'd enjoy going out again."

The men looked to their foreman. "We're just a few hours from here and we do have the two days off. Let's do it."

Chad untied the ribbon as he looked over at Amy, both of them remembering the last gift he got from the crew at Fergis. He removed the wrapping. It was a chain saw. On the top was a bronze plate with his name on it. Chad smiled. "Very useful," he said as he pulled it out entirely. As he put the box on the floor he felt a weight at the bottom as another box slid from one corner to the other. He tipped the box and the other gift fell out.

"Oh no. You guys didn't." He quickly unwrapped and opened the grey velvet box. It was a Stauer. On the back was inscribed his name and Amy's along with their wedding date and a simple best of everything wish. He put on the watch and thanked the men warmly.

"I think Bosley is gone, Amy. No mistaking who I am now," he said.

She got up from the table, walked to the other side and kissed him on the cheek.

He held up his wrist and said, "I see by my brand new watch that we have to go. Thanks, everyone. Enjoy your time at the Cliffside. Amy and I are on our way." He took her by the elbow and led her out of the room.

Chapter 72

Dr. Donna Worden sat next to Kathy at the reception desk. They were going over the appointments for the following week.

"Remember, Kathy, nothing on Monday. Use the day to catch up on paper work and field calls. Dr. Craig will cover for us Wednesday, Thursday and Saturday. Dr. Fisher will be here Tuesday and Friday. Neither of them can work on Thursday afternoon, though. Work appointments around their schedules, okay?"

"No problem, Dr. Worden. I can use the extra time to work on the new program Mr. Harcher sent us." Kathy jotted notes in the appointment book.

Sam came out of the back of the clinic. "That was it for today. If that kid, Robbie, wants to come in to use the equipment after school, Kathy, remind him it's for an hour and he must have a buddy with him. He'll do it, but remind him. He wants his knee in top shape for the football season, so he knows what to do, but not alone, okay?" He hung up the white lab coat next to Donna's.

"Let's go, girl. We have to make the Greentree Inn in Pittsburg by eight p.m." "If you let me drive, we'll make it by six," she smiled up at him. "Are you sure it's all right for both of us to go? I could stay here at the clinic and you could fly out to your board meeting."

"Absolutely not. We've been working too hard, both of us. We need a break to re-energize. Doctor's orders, Doctor."

"Yes, Doctor." They both laughed at their silliness.

"I want my co-recipients of the scholarship to see how well I'm doing. And they need to meet the prettiest ortho-specialist on the east coast, my fiancée and lover," Sam said as he patted her knee.

"Flattery will get you everywhere. Put the pedal to the metal, sir, and aim this Buick right for the Greentree Inn." She flashed her even white teeth.

He was quiet a moment as he drove along. "I just wish my father could see how things worked out."

Donna put her hand over his on the steering wheel. "He saw the beginning of it all, and I'm sure he's looking down and smiling at the rest of it."

"Yeah, I hope so. Well, at least it's nice to have my Mom around. She gets a kick out of all the equipment, doesn't she?" Sam beamed.

"Shirley is a doll. When she visits the first thing I ask Kathy to do is make a fresh pot because I know your Mom doesn't show up empty handed. Those pastries are dynamite."

"Did you hear Kathy when we said we were going away? She said she gets to pick from the pastries first for a change." Donna chatted on. "I have a deal with Shirley…whenever she gets to the office, she comes to me first, so I can choose what I want. Otherwise the patients clean her out in no time. It drives Kathy crazy when your Mom passes the desk and heads to the back office."

"Well," said Sam, "I'd hate to see Kathy overdo it. I need to have her stay as shapely as she is. She's a good first impression at the reception desk."

"Kathy uses the exercise equipment whenever we're not around. Her arms and her pecs are doing just fine and that's about all the time I want to spend talking about that blond receptionist, thank you," Donna said with fake envy.

"You hired her, love," he giggled at her. "Anyway, I do like to see Mama responding so well to her therapy. She's lost almost all the swelling at her ankles and she walks a lot better."

"We'll keep her going as long as we can, Sam. She's a strong woman full of sound advice and I find myself turning to her more and more when I need someone to listen to my prattle. So what do I expect to find in Chicago?" Amy held her left hand out in front of her and let the sun catch the diamonds on her third finger. She turned it left and right and watched it cast prisms along the dashboard.

Sam laughed a deep throaty rumble. "For one thing, people who will adore that ring, and you, too, sweetie. These are real folks who work hard just like we do. I can't wait to show you off. Did you bring that little red dress with the skinny straps?"

"Sure did, my man. Sure did."

"All five of us were poor students who knew we had to work extra hard if we were ever going to accomplish our goals. This Romans/ Burkas Foundation showed us the way and then some. Today, we can all say we did what we set out to do and the foundation made it all possible for us to make it happen in a relatively short period of time. I want you to like these people, Donna. They will always be a part of our lives."

She put her arm through his an leaned her head on his shoulder. "I love them already because they enabled you to come to UCLA when you did and you, sir, have saved my life. I'll be eternally grateful. I love you Sam Carter and I want to marry you and you can consider that a proposal from this modern woman who is just a little tired of waiting for you to say those words."

He pulled the car onto the shoulder of the interstate, put it in park, turned to Donna and put his arms around her, kissing her deeply.

"I don't know what to say, except a hearty yes, yes, yes."

Chapter 73

They all sat around the sun porch at the Romans' house in Bluff View. Sam and Donna got there first, followed by Barry Kretzler, Hal Jensen and Michele Banks, the Andrews and finally, Amy and Chad. The lights around the bay sparkled across the silvery waters. Summer boaters skimmed across the moon's reflection.

Donna stood by the window. "This is a breathtaking view. I can't get enough of it."

Marie Andrews joined her. "When I first came here I was the same way. The first night I ever spent here was on this porch, all night. I was born and raised in Pennsylvania, so huge bodies of water like this one were a fascination for me."

Donna stared at Marie. "And I can't believe that I'm standing here next to the Marie Andrews, a celebrity of such stature. I am so thrilled. You and your husband bring such joy with your music and documentaries."

"Sam, how did you find this gorgeous creature? I thought I was the only lucky man on the planet." Hal wrapped his arm around Michele. She blushed.

"I know five lucky people on this ol' Earth, my man. And here we are." Sam kissed Donna on the neck.

"What time do we meet tomorrow? Is it nine or nine-thirty?" Marie sipped her wine.

"Nine-thirty," said Barry. "Ridley emphasized the word 'sharp'."

"Hey," whispered Sam conspiratorially. "He's something else, you know. I asked for a few bucks to buy a ring for my lady and he put a cap on it."

"You mean it could have been bigger?" Donna's eyes were squinty, her arms akimbo.

Everyone laughed. Marie said, "Don't get me started on that subject. He has us all on a short leash."

"But it was always for our own good. Now, I see us all on firm ground. Soon we'll be masters of our own financial ships." Amy stretched in the recliner.

"Don't count on it, Dr. Crowley." Brian Harcher stood in the doorway. They shook hands all around. It seemed that everyone needed a few moments with Brian to clarify some computer program or other.

But first, Amy reminded Brian of her new status. "I'm Dr. Fergis now, sir. Meet Chad, my brandy new hubby."

"We are all happy to see you doing so well, Chad." Brian was graying nicely, Amy noticed.

"You know, Amy, when I heard about you and Chad, I thought of the time you saved my life on the boat, the *Eva*, remember?" Sam asked from across the room.

"That's my girl, Sam." Chad gave a thumbs up.

Brian sat beside Sam and Donna. They talked orthopedic programs. Brian made promises to send more. And so it went into the night.

Chapter 74

The five fresh candidates for the Romans-Burkas scholarship filed into the room. They looked wide-eyed, nervous and very familiar to the original five who sat across from them at the long mahogany conference table. Brian was there, as was Jacqueline Kasinsky, Lisa and Edward Karetsky and Michael Ridley. The Randals and Ingrahms were gone, as well as Muriel and Ada. But their grant money lived on. Romans-Burkas was part of their estates now.

Their thoughts went back to that day that changed their lives so drastically. Marie and Amy were strong women now, bonded with solid marriages. Hal, Barry and Sam metamorphosed into confident, professional, responsible young men. They watched the three girls and two boys who would soon begin their journeys sustained by the foundation and controlled by Ridley and Karetsky. All five knew that they had been correctly led every step of the way.

Ever the lawyer, Barry stood and said, "I speak for the five of us. If any of you ever need any of us to help you in any way, our numbers are in your folders. We'd like to make it as easy for you as we can, but, you'll be facing long hours and hard work. Believe us, it's all worth the pain."

The morning was draining. The board filed out and went, as once before, to the Lakeside Inn for lunch. They knew the elated candidates would join them in about an hour, totally brainwashed by Ridley and Karetsky.

"How long are you staying in Chicago?" Barry asked Amy as they stood against the large window at the Lakeside.

"Just overnight. Chad and I are on our honeymoon, you know."

"Nice match, kiddo. I really mean that. You two were made for each other." He sipped at some lemon water. Outside the dining room windows the noon sun glinted off the waves gently blown up by a soft breeze. Dozens of boats made their way out of the bay.

"Barry, we were long ago and we each served a purpose for the other...."

"Hey, Amy, come on. That was a century ago. We're entirely different people now. We were really using each other, right? But in a nice way, don't you think?"

He's a real lawyer now, Amy noticed. So professional, so confident, so right. They did use each other and their relationship had served a useful purpose.

They were both in the right place at a right time in their lives.

"How is Jenna?"

"Almost due. That's why I'm headed back tomorrow morning. Hal and Michele will be coming with me to look at a lot we bought. Right Hal?" He leaned over and looked down the table at Hal.

"Sure enough. We'll see what kind of shack we can put on his three acres. Is anyone up for a boat ride this afternoon? I was thinking of the five of us like the last time we were all here." Hal raised his eyebrows questioningly.

Marie broke off a piece of roll and muttered, "Not exactly like last time, I hope."

"Sam, you game?" asked Amy with a smug smile.

"Only if you go along, Doc. Only if you go along."

"It's all set, then. Just the five of us. Our guests can lounge around, see the sights, or whatever. But this afternoon we'll reprise our first trip." Barry was bright-eyed.

Chapter 75

They drifted along the coastline, past the Veterans' Home, along piers jutting out into the serene Lake Michigan. And they talked. They recounted their experiences to each other, their plans for the future, even their setbacks, the tragedies and those with whom they now shared their lives..

Barry finished his beer. "Hey, Sam. Stand by the rail while I turn this boat around." He laughed fiendishly.

Marie squealed. "Amy, get ready."

Sam rolled his eyes. He thought about that day when he fell into the lake and all the good fortune he's had since then.

"Know what? When I get married, probably in June of next year, would you all come here to my wedding? My Donna deserves nothing but the best and you are the best, we are the best. Here's to us." He raised his bottle of beer.

"I speak for all of us, Sam because I see what's in everyone's face. We will be here no matter what is going on in our lives. That's a solemn promise."

The sun was starting to set. The brightness was fading to soft hues of orange, red and lavender. The group headed for the Romans' dock, probably for the last time together since they were each becoming parts of their own families, families that would continue to grow. The boat glided gracefully into its slip, the five holding on to the rail or the mast.

A great blue heron, stretched straight as an arrow, spread its wide wings over the boat, circled slowly and wheeled west, a silhouette in the setting sun.

Printed in the United States
56375LVS00005B/345